SII

By the same author
STORM SURGE
QUINTIN'S MAN
THE MISSING GERMAN
THE SPECTRUM
LANDSLIP
THE FERRYMAN
RISKS
THE EXETER BLITZ
IN THE TENT

David Rees

SILENCE

LONDON : DENNIS DOBSON

Copyright © 1979 by David Rees
All rights reserved

ESSEX COUNTY LIBRARY
JF

First published in Great Britain in 1979
by Dobson Books Ltd, 80 Kensington Church Street, London W8
Printed in Great Britain by
Bristol Typesetting Co. Ltd., Bristol

ISBN 0 234 72095 6

CV 93714

For
David Milton

The sound of silence
  is all the instruction
you'll get
  —Jack Kerouac, *Desolation Angels*

The songs of Simon and Garfunkel are published
by Pattern Music Ltd.

ONE

It was the worst time of his life. He should have seen it coming; it was bound to happen sooner or later. He had always been too lucky. Kim started the Simon and Garfunkel track for the fifth time: Hello darkness, my old friend.

'You'll wear that thing out,' said his mother, coming into the room with his mug of cocoa. 'Haven't you any homework?'

'No.'

She sighed. 'All you seem to do these days is listen to that record. Why don't you go out for a walk?'

He stretched out on his bed. 'Yes, I probably will.'

'No sugar, as you wanted.' She left.

Silence like a cancer grows.

Yes, he thought, he had always been too lucky. The gang of friends at primary school, friends all the way through the comprehensive, not like some poor lonely sods. Maybe Mum and Dad left a few things to be desired: they weren't the sort of parents it was easy to talk to. But he got on with them well enough. They didn't stop him going out, or complain about long hair or loud pop music. It was just that they seemed so set in their ways; the trivialities of life were all that interested them. He couldn't imagine them as young lovers. They were all right, though. He could always turn to them if the worst ever came to the worst.

School work was usually within his grasp, was never boring. He was seventeen now, nearly eighteen, in the sixth form, following a course he wanted to do and found he liked: 'A' level maths, physics and chemistry. He was fortunate there too. And in other ways. He was good at games. He wasn't that ugly. He glanced in the mirror to make sure. No, particularly now the spotty phase had disappeared, and some girls seemed to like you tall, with dark hair and brown eyes. Other boys developed so late; at sixteen they still looked like thirteen-year-olds, small, with high voices. What chance did they have in life, indifferent at games, ignored by the girls, no friends? Yes, he had always had it easy.

You often did, someone once remarked to him, until you fell in love or discovered sex. That's when the real problems start. He had laughed at the idea as an absurd generalization; the opposite could just as well be true. It could mean freedom, happiness, adulthood. But he discovered he had been wrong. Judith Irwin was the strangest girl in the school; everybody said so. Avoid her; she's trouble. But it had to be her. They'd been in the same class since the age of eleven, but he had never taken much notice of her then. She was a withdrawn moody person, frequently in trouble because of bad work or skipping lessons, and, in any case, when he was eleven, twelve, he'd been much more interested in his gang of male friends and their various crazes, balsa wood aeroplanes, cycle rides, swopping stamps. But one day, when he was fourteen—he remembered it clearly—he had looked at her differently. She was staring out of the window, gazing at nothing in particular. Something seemed to shift inside him, like a car changing gear, and he knew nothing would ever be quite the same again; he had slid into a new phase of existence.

It was a moony, silly sort of puppy-love; he could see that now. It passed, and he thought another girl would interest him. That seemed to happen with his friends, but it didn't with him. The emotions changed, but they stayed with Judith. And it was all quite useless; she wasn't interested. When she became aware of his feelings, she giggled and whispered about him. He was hurt, and he thought she enjoyed seeing him hurt. Occasionally he spoke to her; she was off-hand or openly rude, and it was like a slap in the face. She went out with other boys, though she was never serious with any of them. Kim accepted this, in a resigned passive sort of way. It was only when they were both sixteen and it was rumoured that Judith had been to bed with at least two or three of her boyfriends that he began to feel the first wild stabs of jealousy. The rumours weren't true, he told himself; boys always thought they had to invent that kind of thing to prove, for some reason or other, that they were more irresistible or more experienced than their friends. How far did you get with so-and-so last night? As if the girl in question was a winning-post in a race, not a person.

Yet he knew he was, in a way, being hypocritical. He went out with a girl occasionally, not perhaps just to be seen with her, but because it was fun: to parties, discos. He loved dancing. And there was one who fancied him, Anna; he led her on, though she didn't need much persuasion. The first time it happened was in the park, on the way home from school. He felt ashamed afterwards; there were no feelings involved. A few months later he stopped it all. It was making him completely confused. He was more than ever in love with Judith. The rumours about her were true, he began to realize. She was quite wild. She had left school at the end of the fifth year, and he saw nothing of her now, though he often walked past her flat late at night, hoping to catch a glimpse of her, maybe even meet her in the street on her way home. But these nocturnal vigils were fruitless. He never saw her. Stories about her reached his ears. Someone had seen her at the cinema, or in a car with a man. She was into the drug scene. She was in trouble with the police, something to do with stealing. He read the local paper, but there was no news of it. It all upset him. He didn't want to love a girl like her. But he did; he could not help himself.

Then, a week ago, the impossible happened. Sandy Becker was eighteen; he was the oldest boy of Kim's year, the first to reach adulthood. Sandy invited all his friends to a party. Judith was there. For the first time in his life Kim had too much to drink. Judith was completely changed, at least as far as he was concerned. She virtually threw herself at him. She did not dance with anyone else all evening, kept filling his glass. He was bewildered, wanted explanations, but Judith only laughed. It was a warm September night, the last of an Indian summer heat-wave. Sandy's parents were out. Kim found himself at the bottom of the garden, leaning against a tree, kissing Judith. They were hidden from the house: trees, shrubs. Autumn scents in the air, sour dead leaves, michaelmas daisies like stale honey. It must be a dream, he told himself; any moment now he would wake up. He was sick: the alcohol. She laughed, and ran back to the house.

Next day he was acutely depressed. She would never want him after that, not after seeing him so drunk. He stayed in his room, playing Simon and Garfunkel's Greatest Hits, a record he had bought the morning before the party. He ate almost nothing for Sunday dinner. Hello darkness, my old friend. But in the evening he plucked up courage and telephoned her. Yes, she'd love to go out with him.

Last week seemed quite unreal now he looked back on it, another dream, part pleasant, part nightmare. He had to go to school, of course, but for once the hours dragged with appalling slowness; he could not concentrate on anything. Teachers reprimanded him, mildly, for they were unused to such lapses of concentration from him, though Mr Dobson, the physics teacher, guessed that he was in love, and did not persecute him at all. He met Judith every evening outside the shop where she worked. He spent a lot of money, stayed out late. His parents didn't like it; what about his homework, they asked. He didn't have any, he lied. As the week wore on his father's frown increased, and his mother's face grew more anxious. Any day now they would say something.

What he discovered about Judith was far from pleasant. She was selfish in the extreme, bad-tempered like a small child if she didn't get her own way. She didn't love him, probably didn't even like him. She mocked him for being so conventional, being a mummy's boy. He wouldn't try dope, not even a puff. He was a coward, just scared of the trouble it might lead to, she said. But she liked to spend his money: expensive drinks, clubs for dancing. It was crazy, he kept telling himself, quite crazy; she was so unlovable. But he could not help himself, maybe because he felt so sorry for her. Her father she had never known; Mr Irwin had left his wife before Judith was a year old. There had been a succession of 'uncles', most of them unsatisfactory to say the least. One was an alcoholic; another had been sent to prison for fraud. Judith herself had been in trouble more than once: drugs. But she had not actually been charged with any offence. She saw little of her mother these days, and, when she did, they spent most of their time quarrelling. Mrs Irwin worked in the afternoons and evenings, so their paths rarely crossed, except at weekends. Kim wished he could protect her from this sad life, take her off to some remote place where there were just the two of them, and let his love for her bring her back to some saner concept of things. She was such a little waif, a piece of human wreckage.

When they met at half past five they always went back to the flat Judith shared with her mother. This was the best time, but Kim was uneasy that it was the only part of the evening he enjoyed, the two of them in the flat together, alone. She seemed so much more natural than when they went out, content to potter round the place, talk about old acquaintances, the good times at school. Even so it wasn't very satisfying. When he kissed her she always drew away first, didn't really like it. What does she want from me, he asked himself. It was bewildering. And as for anything more than kissing, it was out of the question. He went home frustrated, annoyed even. She could see how he felt, but apparently it only amused her. She wasn't trying to humiliate him deliberately, he imagined, but that was the effect.

Nevertheless, he was always outside the shop at half past five, waiting.

This evening he had come to the shop as usual. Judith was not there. Someone had called for her, a man in a car. Kim, stunned, asked who the man was, where they had gone. The manageress stared at him curiously, and said she hadn't the faintest idea. He went to the flat, but no-one answered the bell. The curtains were drawn. She was in there making love with another man; he was quite convinced of it. He looked to see if there was a strange car nearby, but there were dozens of cars parked up and down the street and any of them could be the right one. Or none of them.

He went home and rang her, but there was no reply. He stayed in and watched television, the programmes scarcely registering on his brain. His parents were upstairs, redecorating their bedroom. He tried to phone again. No luck. A third attempt, and Judith's mother answered. Yes, Judith had gone out. She didn't know where. With someone called Neil. And Judith had asked her to say that Kim was not to ring her, not to call at the shop again. Yes, she'd met someone else, and Kim was to leave her alone.

He returned to the living-room and fell into a chair. His father came in. 'You look fed up,' he said. 'What's the matter?' Kim passed his hands over his face several times, licked his lips.

'Can I have a drink, please, Dad?'

'If you like.'

'A whisky?'

'Yes. Pour one for me, and one for your mother as well. Bring them upstairs.'

He waited a few moments after his father had gone, trying to compose himself. He didn't want any awkward questions. He fixed a smile on his face, and carried the drinks up to the bedroom.

'Who was that on the phone?' his mother asked.

'Oh . . . just someone from school.'

The bedroom looked depressing. His parents were scraping off the wallpaper, and it lay in untidy heaps on the floor. They had taken out the carpet, and covered up most of the furniture with old sheets. The air was full of dust, and there was an unpleasant smell of plaster everywhere. He wondered why they never let him help with jobs round the house. Perhaps they thought he'd be a nuisance; they liked doing these things themselves, and Mum, in particular, was extremely fussy about brushstrokes showing up on the woodwork and drops of paint spilling on the wrong surface.

'Anything good on the telly?' she asked.

'Nothing much.'

'Ah . . . that's a nice drop of scotch,' Mr Hooper said. 'Just what the doctor ordered.'

'It's all right.'

His mother said, 'You're looking a bit off-colour.'

'Oh . . . it's been a tiring day at school. No games with the weather so wet. Cooped up all afternoon indoors.'

She nodded sympathetically. 'I'll bring you in a mug of cocoa when we've finished.' She put her glass down and picked up the scraper. 'Come on, Cliff. Let's get on with this wall. There's only one piece left.'

'Mum . . . no sugar, please. It's fattening.'

'Fattening! *You've* no need to worry! Go out and get some exercise; that's what you want. It's stopped raining.'

'Maybe I will, later.'

His mother was right, he decided. It would do him some good to go out. He took the empty mug downstairs, and said he was in need of fresh air, a stroll round the block.

He walked and walked. Any street, any direction. Purley: always the same dull semi-detached houses, this dormitory suburb on the outskirts of London where he had lived all his life, the same privet hedges and late summer flowers withering in the gardens, the heleniums, the montbretia, the asters. So few people about: families insulated and isolated with their television sets behind shut curtains. There was a little wind and it was chilly: autumn. He avoided the road where she lived. He might have smashed the windows. This jealousy was evil, insidious: he almost wanted to find them in bed together, see their ecstatic faces. What then? Bash them to death with the poker? Parade his hurt? Or a vicarious sexual thrill? He didn't know.

'What's the matter with that boy?' Cliff Hooper asked his wife.

'Nothing much. Why?'

'He seems very fed up tonight.'

'It's his own fault. He never has enough work to do. Out every night last week, and this week all he does is stay in his room listening to that same old record. I don't think they set enough homework at that school, Cliff. I always thought the sixth-form meant swotting hard. It certainly did when I was at school, but everything's changed nowadays.'

'Perhaps he's in love.'

'In love? What on earth makes you say that?' She looked up from the book of wallpaper patterns she was glancing through. As usual, she was never sure that the one they'd finally selected, ordered, and paid for, would be exactly right. Suppose it didn't quite go with the curtains? Or turned out to be too dark? It *was* rather a heavy pattern, she thought.

'It's not uncommon, Beth, for seventeen-year-olds to fall in love.'

'*I* didn't.'

'That's got nothing to do with it.'

'In love? Kim? What does he know about falling in love? He's only a kid.'

'He's not. Not any more.'

'Well . . . who with?' She seemed genuinely perplexed. 'I know he's had girl-friends, but he's never brought one home to meet us. I'd have thought he'd bring her home to meet us if it was serious.'

He heaved himself out of his chair, and came round to look at the pattern book. 'I expect you're right,' he said. 'He likes an evening out, I know, but *I* think he works hard at school, despite what you say. I don't suppose he'll be going steady till he's finished university. If he ever gets there, that is.'

'He's been a bit odd, come to think of it, since that party. Getting drunk at his age! And his bedroom smelling like a brewery!'

'Yes . . . you said quite a lot at the time.'

'Did I? Well, he shouldn't have done it.'

'That's probably why he went out every night last week.'

'Because I was annoyed?'

'Yes.'

'Well, I *was* annoyed. The Beckers should have more sense! Cliff, that stone-coloured pattern, there: I keep wondering if we shouldn't have chosen that.'

'Too late now.'

'Yes. But it's nice and light.'

'You wanted the dark one.'

'I know. Woman's privilege, changing her mind.'

He laughed. 'You did that twice when we were engaged.'

She looked embarrassed. 'I didn't know anything then, did I? No experience of life. No way of telling if I was doing the right thing, marrying you.'

'You were scared.'

She nodded. 'Mum wasn't much help.'

'And did you do the right thing?'

'Of course! Whatever makes you ask? I've never regretted it for a moment! Have you?'

'What makes *you* ask?'

'Well . . . you can be very moody at times. Just like Kim.' She smiled. 'When I was clearing out the bedroom I found the album with our wedding photos. I sat on the floor for half an hour just staring at them! They're going a bit brown now . . . twenty-two years!'

'Where are they?'

'I can't remember. Yes I can; I put them on top of Kim's wardrobe. Do you want to see them?'

'Yes. Why not?'

How awful the fashions were then! It was astonishing how alike people's clothes were; the same drab trousers and jackets on the men, the flowered dresses on the women, quite regardless of whether the style or cut suited a particular individual or not. And the hair! Was it really so short? All those unattractive ears sticking out! But it didn't matter; here were friends and relatives enjoying themselves, looking really happy: the big occasion, their wedding. He'd just finished his National Service. That was something the young didn't have to put up with today. Two wasted years of your life. People said they were mad to get married at their age, both only twenty-one. It was a dull era, the mid-fifties. He remembered the pop songs of the time, all those ballads... *Blue star, when I am blue*... Peggy Lee singing *Mister Wonderful*...Ruby Murray; *Softly, softly, turn the key*... they'd danced to all those, he and Beth. *Hey there! You with the stars in your eyes... It's cherry pink and apple blossom white.* Mambos. Kim wouldn't even have heard of a mambo, let alone know how to do it. Probably think it was a snake. But, in some indefinable way, life was easier then, even if the Egyptians were busy nationalizing the Suez Canal and the Russians were invading Hungary. No drugs problem, for instance. Full employment. Harold Macmillan; you've never had it so good. Relationships weren't so complicated. Of course there was always A who was in love with B who was in love with C who was in love with A; that kind of whirligig had always existed, always would, but there was none of this feeling you were on the shelf if you were still a virgin at sixteen, no television advertising to make you think you'd never get a girl unless you used a certain type of deodorant, none of this should we live together because some other boy and girl are doing so, and men changing nappies and cooking all the meals while the women burned their bras and demonstrated about abortion. You talked about sex, but you didn't have the problem of deciding whether to go all the way or not. Even if you both wanted to (and who didn't?) it was simpler in the long run not to, knowing how risky it might be if you did. You met a nice girl, went out, got engaged, got married, and in most cases no sex before the wedding night. You knew where you were even if it often seemed difficult. He hadn't been allowed at seventeen to stay out so late as Kim, nor so often, and not be asked what he'd been doing. Nor did he have so much money; Saturday jobs were unheard of. Kim had a freedom he'd never known. He was envious, up to a point, but he didn't envy the complexities his son's generation had to face.

'You're deep in thought,' Beth said.

'Remembering.'

'What?'

'The good times past.'

Kim's key turned in the lock, but he didn't come into the lounge. Went straight upstairs to his bedroom. Most peculiar. They could hear him getting undressed; shoes, plonk, plonk, thrown onto the floor, belt buckle hitting the chair. Bed-springs creaking.

There is a girl in it, Mr Hooper thought, and she's a problem. No doubt about it. Well, these things happen. He'll get over it.

TWO

Neil Berry was twenty-two, sold spices for a large firm, and had a smart new car. He shared a house with another young man; he was slight in build, had a moustache and thinning blond hair, and though he was not very good-looking he had plenty of money. This much Kim found out during the next few weeks by asking questions of the right people, and from his own observation. Most days he kept watch at half past five on the shop where Judith worked, hiding in a convenient doorway, or he hovered at night outside the flat. He had seen Neil, in consequence, several times: what could Judith find in him, he wondered; he looked such a complete weed. He himself was better-looking he was certain; sexier too. He examined himself in the mirror after a bath one evening. Not perfect, but surely not unreasonable. However, he had learned that it wasn't necessarily beauty or sex appeal that attracted girls; the week with Judith had taught him that.

It was a strange life he was leading, he thought. At school he found he could just about concentrate on his work, and he was surprised that it was so. Mr Dobson, however, noticed a difference, and often looked at him with a worried expression. But Kim got by without causing comment: the particular experiments they were doing in physics were unusually interesting, and there was enough to do at school to pass the time, with friends and acquaintances, the football season: the day was invariably full. But Judith came into his head frequently, always producing that same sickening lurch, the same faltering of the heart-beats. It was odd, he reflected, how the emotions, whether they were stabs of grief or jealousy, or the happy excitement of knowing you were meeting your beloved in a few hours' time, produced identical sensations, the racing of the blood, the downward rush in the stomach: though what had once been a delight to experience, the joy of knowing you were alive, in touch and in harmony with all things, that existence had point and meaning, now indicated the opposite. He felt cut off from all that was desirable; he was left out of the party, left behind in the race, and nothing, himself in particular, was really alive, had point or meaning any more.

After school was the worst. It became a routine, this solitude in which he allowed, almost pleasurably, his hurt to grow, his wounds to fester. There was the wait outside the shop, then tea at home when he talked desultorily about this and that with his parents, and afterwards the evenings alone in his bedroom. He did his homework, but without enthusiasm; it was adequate, but never really good now. The Simon and Garfunkel he played endlessly; it was full of fragments that now had a significance that had previously escaped him.

> Are you going to Scarborough fair?
> Parsley, sage, rosemary and thyme.
> Remember me to one who lives there
> She once was a true love of mine.

When the weather was fine he wandered about the streets, always trying to avoid passing the flat, never succeeding. That moment when he said to himself, yes, I will walk by the flat, was a pleasure in itself; happiness flooded him almost as if he were actually going to meet her. And after he had gone by, and seen that the rooms were in darkness, the sense of loss was as distressing as that phone call with her mother: 'She's gone out with someone called Neil.' Tomorrow, he said to himself, perhaps tomorrow, I'll see her. The pattern of the streets became part of his life. Pine Gardens, Raeburn Avenue, Alexandra Drive, Northcote Avenue, Southcote Avenue, Endway, Queens Drive, Greenfield Avenue, Elgar Avenue. Great estates of nineteen-thirties semis, monotonous drab boxes where people led indistinguishable lives of eating, watching television and sleeping. You hardly ever saw them; behind their drawn curtains they ate, watched television and slept. Perhaps in some there were wild orgies being held; in one a man might be writing the most magnificent poetry of the twentieth century; in another someone might be on the point of discovering the greatest advance ever made in nuclear physics. Exquisite pleasures, profound satisfaction. But it seemed very unlikely.

He began to notice the differences. No pair of semis was exactly the same. A garish front door, an extra bedroom over the garage, some where people had created gardens with loving dedication, one where the original windows had been replaced with a single sheet of glass. But the differences were superficial: essentially there was the same semi-circle of chairs facing a television, which, the inhabitants probably never realized, formed a complete ring of chairs with the other semi-circle in the adjacent house. Only a wall split the circle in two. This is Your Life. Are You Being Served? Kojak. The News at Ten. Everywhere.

Her road, King Charles Road, was different. It was on the edge of the old town, a street of big Victorian houses that had seen better days; now the multitude of dustbins, the overgrown gardens, the collection of bells by the front doors showed that few were inhabited by just one family. They were flats, bedsitters for the more mobile section of the population; students, foreigners, remnants of broken-up families like Judith and her mother. And, here, in the third week of his prowling, he saw them. He had just turned a corner, and there they were, so near he almost bumped into them. 'Hullo Judith,' he mumbled, and stepped aside into the gutter to let them pass. 'Who's that?' he heard Neil say. They were holding hands. 'Oh, someone I knew vaguely at school,' she answered, and they were round the corner, out of sight. The shock was so great that Kim sat down on a garden wall, his head in his hands. It was several minutes before he felt he was capable of standing up and walking on.

At home, late at night, he talked with his parents over a cup of cocoa. The usual platitudes; the weather, what he'd missed on the television that evening, what was going on at school. Sometimes he had a great urge to tell them what was going on inside him, but it was quite impossible. They wouldn't begin to understand.

'You're getting thin,' his mother said on one occasion. 'You're not eating enough.'

'Growing pains,' he muttered.

'Great big lad like you ought to have three meals a day. How tall are you now?'

'Six feet. Six whole feet of man.' He thumped his fists on his chest, but she wasn't amused.

'You'll make yourself ill if you don't eat more. What was wrong with that chop I cooked this evening?'

'Nothing. I just didn't fancy it.'

'Why not?'

How relentless she could be! 'I just didn't, that's all.' He sighed.

'Waste of good food.'

'I'm sorry.'

'Macaroni cheese tomorrow. Do you think you'll be able to eat that?'

'I expect so.' She did not answer; the inquisition was over. 'Goodnight,' he said.

'Throw your football things downstairs, will you? They ought to go in the washing-machine if you want them clean for Wednesday.'

'Yes Mum.'

Were they ever young, he wondered. Television, jobs round the house: that was all they seemed to live for. What was Mum like at seventeen? He tried to imagine her on a typical evening out, dancing quicksteps and sambas, kissing her boy-friend goodnight. It was impossible to visualize.

It was usually hours before he slept, and then often only after the mattress and the pillow had become Judith: he would press his eyes, his tongue, into the unresponsive cotton; those kisses were better than none, and there was always the one moment of release, of total disappearance into the fantasy Kim and Judith, not at all like the reality. But it only lasted a few seconds, and then he was by himself again, sweating and panting, thinking those spurts of pleasure were just waste. He wished he could go out and find another girl: but the procedure involved in deliberately seeking a partner, the time spent dithering on the edge of a disco sizing one up, the routines of conversation, the lack of any genuine pleasure to be found in it except for the one obvious thing, seemed infinitely wearisome, fraught with complications. When he did sleep, he was restless, waking from dreams in which Judith was dancing or having sex with Neil, and the day saw him rise, listless and grey-faced. In the sleepless hours jealousy was at its most powerful. He struggled against this most disgusting of all the emotions, telling himself that it warped everything, destroyed all the good in himself, that this solitary twisted bitterness was pathetic and ludicrous. But he constantly lost, and in his mind he got the better of Neil in a fight, or by words, or killed him in a variety of ways, and, most disturbing of all, he punished Judith for what she had done to him. This last was a fantasy that repelled him in that it revealed how close love was to hate, how it turned into a sick desire to cause physical pain. He was revolted by the nastiness he discovered inside himself.

The only comfort was Simon and Garfunkel. Like a bridge over troubled water I will ease your mind. In the naked light I saw ten thousand people, maybe more. And the words of the prophet are written on a subway wall. I have no need of friendship; friendship causes pain. It's laughter and it's loving I disdain. Oh I love you, girl. A jumble of rags and tags that brought a kind of peace.

One evening Judith did not come out of the shop, and Neil did not arrive in his car. Next day there was again no sign of them. Kim felt almost annoyed. The routine had been disturbed, and there was no explanation. Even this one daily glimpse of her had been taken away from him.

On the third evening he was lost in *I am a rock* when the bedroom door opened and his mother came in. 'Telephone,' she said.

He turned the volume down. 'Who is it?'

'Neil somebody.'

'Neil! Neil who?' He stared at her, bewildered.

'I don't know, dear. I didn't ask.'

He ran down stairs and picked up the receiver. 'Kim Hooper,' he said.

'Thank God I've found you! It's taken ages, so many more Hoopers in the phone book than—'

'What do you want?'

'Haven't you heard?'

'Heard what?'

'Look, I'd better meet you somewhere. You might know something, some little thing, any detail—'

'What are you talking about?'

'Judith, of course. She disappeared three days ago. You didn't know? Her mother's frantic with worry. She's taken all her clothes... she was last seen getting on a London train. The police have been told, but they've found nothing, no trace. I just thought... well, perhaps you had some idea.'

'Me? I'd be the last person, don't you think, in the circumstances?'

'Kim, don't take that attitude. You were with her before me; I know all about it. I took her away from you and I can guess how much that hurts. But we ought to be thinking of Judith.'

'Yes... yes, of course.' This man definitely seemed to care about her; he couldn't be all bad as Kim had imagined. 'What do you suppose I can do?'

'I've no idea, quite honestly. But... well, two heads I thought... will you meet me in the Globe? In the lounge bar. Do you know it?'

'Yes.'

'In ten minutes' time?'

'Yes. All right.'

'Kim... thanks.' He sounded really grateful. 'We must try and find her. Will you help me?'

'Of course I will. What do you think... where do you think she is?'

'She's probably with some group, some commune, I don't know. The London drug scene.'

'I knew she smoked. Nothing worse.'

'It *is* worse. Acid, hash.'

'I never . . . never even guessed.'

'I think that one week with you . . . I don't know, she really wanted to stop. But it didn't work out.'

'She never said. I wish she'd said.'

'We both love her.' He did not answer. 'We'll find her, bring her home.'

'It's Friday. There's the weekend; I've half-term next week. Yes, we could. Go to London you mean?'

'Yes.'

'We'll talk it over in the pub. I'll see you in ten minutes.'

Mr Hooper was in the Globe that evening. At about nine o'clock he had called on a neighbour, Bill Meadows, to ask his advice on unscrewing a wash-basin. Bill Meadows was a plumber and had the necessary equipment. Mrs Hooper wanted the basin removed: it was enamel and over the years it had got badly chipped; she had bought another one, porcelain, in a soft shade of green that matched the new bedroom wallpaper very nicely. Bill was out, Mrs Meadows said; he was always in the Globe Friday nights. Well, it would make a change, Mr Hooper thought, to have a drink in there. Beth was watching a programme he didn't fancy, and there was nothing else to do now that he couldn't fix the basin.

When he looked through into the other bar he was surprised to see Kim. His son was breaking the law, not yet eighteen and drinking in a pub. It was a silly law, of course. You could be had up for buying half a bitter, but you were allowed to drive a car. It didn't make sense. Seventeen was an odd age, though; you were neither a kid nor an adult. Bound to be anomalies. He tried to recall his own seventeen-year-old self but found it was difficult. The Festival of Britain. Churchill had just become Prime Minister for the second time. Sweets were still rationed. Certainly he had drunk in pubs when he was Kim's age, but he wished Kim wouldn't do so in the Globe. It was too near home; people would know. Tony Austin, who lived a few doors up from the Hoopers, was a policeman; suppose he came in? It would be different out in the countryside, of course. He and Beth had taken Kim into a village pub before now. No-one had asked any questions and the boy passed easily enough for eighteen, drank his beer like a man.

Who was that he was talking to? A deep earnest conversation: these youngsters trying to settle all the wrongs of the world, as usual. The friend was older, already grown up; not someone from school, he guessed. Do you want the other half, Bill Meadows asked. Yes, he replied; please. Beth's programme wouldn't be over yet, and he had a sudden feeling of depression as he thought of tomorrow: a trip down to Pevensey to see his mother-in-law. Another beer would be very pleasant. When he looked up again Kim and his friend had gone.

Beth seemed rather short-tempered. Perhaps she was annoyed he'd stayed out so long; he hadn't said he was going to the Globe. 'What's the matter?' he asked.

'Nothing much. Kim.'

'Why, what's he done?'

'He says he's not coming to Pevensey. He's going up to London to stay with some friends for two or three nights.

I don't know who these friends are or anything about them, but he was most insistent; said it was half-term and he needed a good break. I said it was just as good a break going to Pevensey. Mother always looks forward to seeing him; she'll feel so let down. He could have a nice long walk by the sea and a bit of fresh air in his lungs. It would make a nice change. But he wouldn't listen. Said there was nothing for him to do down there; he'd be bored stiff. He's rude and ungrateful I think.'

Mr Hooper felt very disappointed. He could see Kim's point of view; these trips to Pevensey were exceedingly dull for both of them. All Grandma could talk about was her aches and pains, and what her cat had been doing during the week. Beth never seemed to mind. She was devoted to her mother who was a lonely widow with few friends. He and Kim often went out on these occasions, to the beach or high up on the cliffs near Seaford, leaving the two women to natter. Beth liked to do the housework for the old lady, or some shopping or cooking; yes, Kim was right: nothing much for him to do down there. 'You could have stopped him,' he said. 'Why didn't you?'

'And have him sulk and be generally unpleasant all week-end? No thank you.'

'What's he going to do in London that he can't do from here? It's not exactly a long journey from Purley station to Victoria.'

'I don't know. He was very vague about it.'

'What about his Saturday job?'

'He'd already arranged with Mr Rice not to go into the shop this week as we're going to Pevensey.'

'I wonder what's he's up to.'
'What do you mean?'
'Perhaps there's a girl in it.'
'Do you think so?'
'There might be.'
'He said he's going with a Neil somebody or other.'

Up till now Mr Hooper had thought Kim was too sensible to get entangled with a girl, what with work for 'A' levels, and wanting a university place. He approved of what he guessed were his son's priorities; if the boy was clever enough to read for a degree he wouldn't stand in his way. It was something he'd like to have done himself. But he hadn't forgotten everything about being seventeen; this girl, if she existed, was mixed up in this London business somewhere. But it would not be a good idea to pursue such a line of thinking with Beth; she'd really start worrying. 'He's old enough to look after himself,' he said.

'I daresay he is,' she answered. 'I'm not scared he'll come to any harm. He'll probably enjoy himself, a football match then a film in the evening. That's the sort of thing he likes doing. You know what he is for old films. I just wish he didn't find it so easy to let Mother down, that's all. It's so selfish.'

'Yes. I suppose it is.' Mr Hooper thought how much more uninteresting tomorrow would be without Kim. It wasn't that they ever discussed anything exciting together; on a three-mile walk they might exchange only a few words about the scenery, or go over last week's football for a bit, or complain mildly about Grandma, but their silences were, he'd always felt, companionable ones. Father and son didn't necessarily have to indulge in profound conversations; after all, they'd lived in the same house for nearly eighteen years. But it began to occur to him that perhaps those silences weren't quite as companionable as he'd imagined, that perhaps Kim was bored stiff not just with Grandma, but with his parents. 'It's not lively enough for him,' he said. 'Maybe we're too old-fashioned and dull.'

'Whatever do you mean, Cliff?' Mrs Hooper was surprised. She was tidying away newspapers, taking dirty cups out to the kitchen, putting the house straight before going to bed. She stopped in her tracks.

'Well... we never do anything very thrilling, do we? Not from his stand-point. He doesn't find his amusements with us. He's growing up, beginning to lead his own life. We're not part of it.'

'That's awful!' She cleaned an ash-tray rather vigorously, and put it back in its proper place, an inch to the right of the television. 'And I don't think it's true.' Mr Hooper said nothing. 'I always imagined we were a close family, happy and united.'

'So we are.' What had he done now, he asked himself. He shouldn't have opened his big mouth.

'You just said we weren't. I thought this was a happy home to live in; God knows I do my best to please both of you! Now it seems it's not good enough.'

'I didn't say that.'

'You did.'

Mr Hooper sighed, and knocked out his pipe. 'All I said was... oh, it doesn't matter.'

The key clicked in the front door, and Kim came in. 'You're late,' his mother snapped.

He glanced at his watch, surprised. 'Five past eleven,' he said. 'I'm not going to school tomorrow.'

'And you stink of beer.' Mr Hooper signalled to him not to say anything. 'I'm off to bed,' she announced, and walked out of the room.

'What was all that about?' Kim asked.

'Nothing.'

'Me going to London, I suppose.'

'No. No, it wasn't.'

'Oh?' He hovered, uncertainly, in the doorway, hoping his father would say more. But when it was obvious that Dad would not, he said 'I'll go up, too. I'm tired.'

'Kim. Is everything all right?'

'Yes.' Whatever was he driving at? 'Why shouldn't it be?'

'You've been a bit moody lately. Is it . . . a girl?'

He hesitated. His father had never asked him such a question before. 'Yes,' he said.

'Do you want to talk about it?'

He felt acutely embarrassed. The idea of telling his father, of all people, the whole Judith saga, even in a watered-down version, was quite intolerable. 'I'd . . . rather not,' he said. 'I'm sorry. That sounds dreadfully rude, I know.'

'I don't want to interfere.'

'No, no . . . you're not interfering.'

'Are you going to London with her?'

'With . . . ? No. I'm not.' Nothing untruthful about

34

that, but he hoped he wasn't blushing. 'It's all over, anyway. I think.'

'Oh.' Mr Hooper fished out the newspaper his wife had tidied away. 'These things happen.'

'Yes.' He watched his father re-lighting his pipe. 'Well ... goodnight, Dad.'

'Goodnight. See you in the morning.'

Mr Hooper sat in the armchair, listening to the sounds of his household going through their usual late-night routine: Kim pulling the lavatory chain, Beth cleaning her teeth, Beth in slippers padding backwards and forwards across the carpet, Kim's feet, louder and slower, making the floorboards groan. Kim banging his bedroom door shut. Well, he had tried, but he'd been told, very definitely, to keep out. There was a whole area, then, of his son's life he knew nothing of, which the boy didn't want him to know of. Nothing wrong in that, but it made him feel old. Why, it was only the other day, or so it seemed, that Kim was a toddler, playing in this room with toy trains, stumbling with words in Ladybird books. He frowned. They didn't communicate, the members of this family, didn't communicate at all, didn't even want to. It was his own fault, probably. Since Kim was about thirteen, there were subjects they'd avoided. They'd drifted into going their own ways. Kim must have been out twice this evening, he realized. Left the pub, come home to tell his mother about London, then ... what? Gone to this Neil to say it was all right, presumably. It wasn't important, being ignorant of these minor details of his son's movements, but ... it made him feel old. He concentrated on the unfinished crossword in the newspaper. Four down. 'Well balanced but apathetic.' Eight letters. What Kim thought of his father, perhaps. Clifford had eight letters. No, it was a nice pun: *listless* was the answer.

THREE

Saturday afternoon, and Kim was in the West End of London, searching. He had a photograph of Judith, a good likeness taken recently, that Neil had given him, a head and shoulders portrait. The first places he visited, amusement arcades, he approached apprehensively, feeling he looked wrong, too wholesome in new jeans and a white Arran sweater. Tomorrow, he thought, he would wear something more scruffy. Unless, of course, he found her today, and that was highly unlikely; looking for a lost girl in London was a hopeless task. An army could disappear without trace here. He stood on the pavement in Piccadilly Circus, gazing at the crowds of people milling about in all directions, the queues of traffic halting at red lights and jerking forward when they changed to green. The arcades were places worth trying, Neil had said. He himself had decided to visit all the hostels where homeless people were taken in; he would meet Kim later, at about seven o'clock, outside the National Gallery, and exchange information.

Kim was very nervous at first, accosting complete strangers who looked, many of them, as if they could easily stick a knife in him, but apart from a few who were annoyed that their pin-table games had been momentarily interrupted, he was treated with relative politeness. Some just glanced for a brief second and shook their heads; others took the photograph and examined it with care before saying they'd never seen her. One or two angrily told him, for reasons he didn't stop to ask, to piss off. One lad, about his own age, said he was certain he had seen her, about a month ago. 'It couldn't have been a month ago,' Kim said. 'She only ran away four days back.'

The boy shrugged his shoulders. 'Please yourself,' he said. The expression on his face turned hostile. 'What do you want to know for, eh? The law?'

'She's my girl-friend. Was.'

'What's wrong with you, then? She just clears off and leaves you.'

Kim moved away, glad to be outside on the pavement in the ordinary crowd. There was a distinctly unpleasant atmosphere about these amusement places. The cheap glitter, the noise, the flickering lights, the shabbiness he expected: the unpleasantness was something to do with the people in there. There were few girls; most of the customers were teenage boys, some of them very young, no more than twelve or thirteen years old. Almost all were alone, and concentrating with immense attention on the machines that took away their cash. Many looked pale and thin, and maybe, like Judith, they had run away to London, thinking that here the excitement of real life was to be found that had been lacking in their dull homes. These arcades, though, were nasty dirty places, rather sinister: there were some queer-looking men in the crowd who gave Kim a shuddery sensation. They hovered, singly or sometimes in pairs, watching the boys, almost like vultures: he wondered what kind of corruption they stood for, what would happen to any of the young kids who might accept their offer of a meal, or a bed for the night.

He walked along the Haymarket, across Trafalgar Square and down to the Embankment Station. Here was a park which was well-known as a hang-out for homeless people, and where drugs surreptitiously changed hands. A policeman watched. Kim hesitated, then decided to explain what he was trying to do; he didn't want to be arrested for soliciting. The policeman nodded, told him to go ahead. The park was full. A few tramps lay asleep on the grass, but otherwise the people who sat on the benches or strolled aimlessly about looked quite ordinary. Perhaps it was the wrong time of day, mid-afternoon. He found a group of youngsters, gentle long-haired types, listening to a boy playing a guitar. They shook their heads, smiling; no, they hadn't seen Judith. Had he tried the hostels? Come back at night; he might have more luck. He walked on, asked a few other people, a bearded man in dirty jeans, a woman with a baby. It was a waste of time.

The same back in Trafalgar Square. He had not thought beforehand that this would be a likely place, but it was full of teenagers leaning against the walls or wandering about doing nothing. They seemed more furtive here, not very anxious to speak, or else they were the wrong sort altogether, people more like himself who, as he might on another occasion, come to Trafalgar Square simply for the purpose of gazing at Nelson or Landseer's huge lions, or staring into the fountains. Someone approached him; would he like to come home for half an hour, the young man wanted to know. What for, he asked. The boy laughed, and walked away. A rent-boy, Kim supposed, watching him stroll back to the place against the wall where he had been standing before.

Then, amazingly, someone said she recognized the girl in the photograph. No, she didn't know Judith's name, but she was quite certain she had seen her last night. At 3, Clifton Square, near Notting Hill Gate tube station. Yes, she'd been round there to see a friend, and that girl was in the house. It was a condemned property occupied by squatters.

He hurried back to the Embankment and took the underground to Notting Hill Gate. He found the right house after a little searching, and though it was in the hands of squatters the front door was wide open. He was surprised; what he knew of such people came from snippets of news on the television: they usually barricaded themselves inside and were very unfriendly towards anyone who wanted to gain entry. The hall, bare of furniture, was filthy, and there was a stench of sweaty bodies and unwashed clothing. A young man came out of the kitchen and Kim explained his errand. No, he didn't think Judith lived here, he said, glancing at the photograph, then added, with a nervous giggle, that he didn't know everybody in the house, or even how many people there were altogether. They came and went so often. The best thing to do was to knock on all the doors and ask.

The first room was empty. The windows had been smashed and boarded up with galvanized tin. There was no electricity. In the dim light he saw that there were several sleeping-bags and a couple of mattresses on the floor, rucksacks, and the inevitable guitar. The smell was awful. In the room opposite a man and a woman lay in bed. He left hurriedly, but they called him back. No, they didn't know Judith. Try upstairs. In the attic he noticed that someone had painted a huge mural of brightly coloured flowers. Two bearded men sat on the floor, sharing a joint. They were so stoned Kim could get no sense out of them. In the next-door room a woman who had a small child with her said that someone who looked very like Judith lived in the house; no, she wasn't the girl in the photograph. This girl was called Nadia and, besides, she'd been there for the past six weeks.

So that was that. He had drawn another blank. He made his way downstairs, and, needing a pee, opened the lavatory door. It was disgusting: no water. He held his breath; if he inhaled that foul air he felt he would choke. He decided to look in the kitchen. No-one there: a cracked ceiling, pipes covered in dirt and cobwebs. A bag of sugar and a kettle on the window-sill. Crude messages scribbled on the walls. As he was going out into the street a man came up the steps. He examined the photograph, turned it over, then peered at it again. 'Have you tried Soho?' he asked.

'No. Why there?'

The man laughed. 'It's a place runaway girls often end up.'

'Oh. I see.' Kim hoped he wasn't blushing.

'I saw someone the other night who looked rather like her.'

'Did you! Do you know her name?'

The man laughed again. 'You just up from the country, son? You don't ask their names.'

Unlikely though it was—it seemed much more improbable than the idea of Judith in a commune of addicts or hippies—it could just be so: if no other clues turned up, it was something they might try. Though the idea of approaching those sleazy women in doorways, saying 'Have you seen the girl in this photograph?' was much more intimidating than stopping passers-by in a park or knocking on doors in a derelict house.

Neil was waiting for him in Trafalgar Square. He, too, had found nothing. 'I need a bath,' he said. 'The places I've been in make me itch.'

'I was thinking it's a high price they pay for freedom. A joint or two to make them feel it isn't really happening. Stench, poverty. God! The kids I've seen! All sorts of weirdos waiting to pounce and exploit them.'

Neil agreed. 'Some of the people who run these hostels are pretty odd. I've seen some nasty types today. And a few Florence Nightingales, I must admit.'

'I really do like the new wallpaper,' Mrs Hooper said, as the car turned into Shingle Drive, the road where her mother lived. 'It may take some getting used to, I'll admit.

The green in it might be too dark. Do you think the green in it might be too dark?'

He smiled. 'No, I don't think the green in it might be too dark.' Colour schemes were something he had decided many years ago not to have an opinion about. Whatever he considered right was invariably over-ruled; it was simpler in the long run to agree with Beth and say nothing, unless she went crazy and chose something unbelievably hideous. Fortunately, however, her taste was not too outlandish.

'What are you smiling at?'

'Us saying "the green in it might be too dark" three times when once was enough.'

'You said it too.'

'One hundred per cent less than you did.'

'What are you talking about?'

'The dark green wallpaper we've bought for our bedroom.'

'Do you think it is too dark, Cliff?'

He laughed. 'No!!'

She looked a bit hurt, and turned away. 'There's Mother on the doorstep.'

Mr Hooper's smile faded. Sometimes, he thought, he would appreciate a wife having a little more sense of humour than Beth.

Grandma was extremely upset. Her cat, Biscuit, had disappeared. He hadn't been seen since yesterday lunchtime, when he'd come in for a piece of whiting and a saucer of milk. He had stayed out all night, which was unheard of, and his breakfast was still in his dish, untouched. He could be lost, run over, dead... There were tears in the old lady's eyes. 'Now, Mother, you come in and sit down,' said Beth, taking charge. 'I'll make you a nice cup of tea. I'm sure he can't be far away.' And Kim wasn't here. What a shame; she'd been so looking forward to seeing him. Young people nowadays always seemed to find something else to do when they were wanted, though Kim wasn't like that of course, not as a rule. She'd been hoping he'd go out and search for Biscuit. 'Don't fret yourself, Mother,' said Beth. 'Cliff will find him for you.'

'Me?'

'Why not?'

'How can I go looking for a lost cat? I wouldn't know where to begin.'

'Oh, Cliff!'

'I can't shout "Biscuit! Biscuit! Where are you?" all over the neighbourhood! People will think I'm raving mad!'

'You don't need to!' She took him aside, and spoke more quietly. 'Humour her, can't you? Have a walk round. I don't suppose you will find him, but... well... go through the motions. She'll be pleased to know we're doing something to help.'

'Oh, all right.' It would at least give him an excuse to get out of the house, he realized.

'Before you start, bring the stuff in from the car, would you? There's a bunch of flowers and a bottle of tonic wine. And that cake I made.'

There was nowhere more dismal than the estate where

his mother-in law lived. The houses looked as if they'd been built of matchwood: some were lean-to shacks that were used as holiday bungalows; the rest were places inhabited only by the old. It was an area where people came to wither and die. Doors and porches were out of all proportion to the size of the walls; there was a forest of television aerials, a web of telephone wires and electric light cables. Hardly anything could grow in the bleak little gardens because the air was so salt. Shingle Drive, Rock Road, Harbour Crescent, Creek Avenue: and you couldn't even see the sea, though it was less than two hundred yards away; a huge ridge of pebbles, thrown up by centuries of high tides, blotted it from view. It was all very different from Purley. The houses there were solid and reassuring, the gardens established, a mass of beautiful flowers in spring and summer. It was customary to mock at suburbia these days, but, really, there wasn't a better sort of life. You were near the country but you had all the facilities of the town, and look at the house prices! That was a sure indication that the suburbs were popular.

Mr Hooper saw only three cats on his walk, and none of them resembled Biscuit, who was a mongrel of uncertain origin, with vague tortoise-shell attachments. An evil-looking tabby eyed him from a comfortable position on a garage roof, and a black and white creature minced in a doorway, washing its face. The third, a mangy marmalade affair, slunk off into a garden when he came near. Mr Hooper didn't like cats. They were unpredictable and unaffectionate, a waste of human time and effort.

He particularly disliked Biscuit, largely because his mother-in-law seemed more fond of the beast than she was of him.

He climbed up the pebble ridge and stared at the sea. It was grey and dull, like the sky. This English Channel sea never did anything very interesting, with its little wavelets lapping pathetically at the edge of the stones, leaving lines of limp seaweed. Give him the Atlantic Ocean in Devon or Cornwall every time, green breakers crashing in cascades of white foam against the rocks!

He wished, again, that Kim was here; the boy would be company, keep his mind off depression. No doubt where Kim was at this minute: in the stadium at Highbury. Arsenal at home to Liverpool. He'd worked it out from the newspaper this morning, and felt quite pleased with himself; at least one of the details of his son's movements he could be certain of. Chelsea, Spurs, West Ham and Queen's Park Rangers were all playing away. Orient or Brentford Kim wouldn't be interested in, and, if he wanted to go to Crystal Palace, it would be an easier trip from Purley than from wherever he was in London. A flat in Camden Town he'd said was where he was staying, but he'd been unhelpful about that too, wasn't sure of the street and had no idea of the phone number when Beth had asked. Millwall, Charlton or Fulham were the only other possibilities, but with the thought of an Arsenal-Liverpool clash they were highly unlikely. He rather wished he was at Highbury himself. He wasn't exactly a fan; followed the results, of course, on television or in the Sunday paper, but he hadn't been to a match for ages.

He'd taken Kim to see Palace a number of times about five years back, but he was glad, really, to let him go off with his friends the following season, and stay at home himself. It was so cold on the terraces in the middle of winter, and standing up for so long...

He looked at his watch, and decided to return to Shingle Drive. It would soon be tea-time. He was hungry; they'd stopped on the way down at a pub in the Ashdown Forest, but he'd only fancied a ham sandwich and half a bitter. The cake Beth had made was inviting; she was a good cook, one of the best.

Half-way along Harbour Crescent, a mongrel cat with tortoise-shell markings streaked across the road, over a garden wall and through the open front door of a bungalow. It was Biscuit, he was certain. He approached tentatively. Suppose it wasn't? He was tempted, for a second, to go on, and forget he'd seen the wretch, but conscience pricked him. It wouldn't be fair on Grandma, blast her. He knocked on the door, and a distraught-looking middle-aged woman came out.

'Er... excuse me... the cat...'

'Oh, is it yours?' Her face broke into a smile of relief. 'I don't know where it came from, but it's in there.' She pointed to the front room. 'It's growling and spitting like a maniac!'

'Is it!' He was more than ever tempted to retreat. 'It isn't mine, but it could be my mother-in-law's. Her cat vanished yesterday morning, and there's been no trace of it since.'

'You're more than welcome to come in and see. The

last thing I want in this house is somebody else's cat!' She ushered him into the front room. There, on the hearth, was Biscuit. Quite definitely.

Feeling rather foolish, Mr Hooper moved slowly towards the animal. 'Biscuit,' he said, in what he considered a very reasonable tone of voice, 'come on now. I'm going to take you home.'

The cat arched its back. At any moment it would run away again, behind the furniture, or between his legs. He would have to grab it, suddenly and unexpectedly. He stood over it, watching. Biscuit glared at him, eyes full of hate. He dived. The cat shot away, over the fender and up the chimney.

'Oh dear!' said the woman. 'Whatever are we going to do now?'

Mr Hooper had an inspiration. Remembering how his mother-in-law persuaded Biscuit in from the garden, he said 'If you'd be so kind . . . a saucer of milk, and a spoon to tap it with. Then I'll call him down.'

'Yes . . . yes.'

'I'm sorry to cause you so much trouble.' He was beginning to get a strong desire to giggle.

Milk and a spoon were fetched, but the only answer to Mr Hooper's entreaties was a scrabbling noise, which seemed to indicate that the cat was climbing up rather than down. He squatted on his hands and knees and peered up the chimney. 'Biscuit!' he shouted. An avalanche of soot fell on his face.

'Oh my goodness!' The woman clapped her hands to her mouth. She, too, was evidently trying not to laugh.

'I should have had that chimney swept in the spring, but I didn't bother. I'm ever so sorry.'

'It's all right. I'll ... er ... go outside. I don't want to shake soot all over your carpet.' He could hardly see.

The woman followed him. 'I'm ever so sorry,' she repeated.

'So am I. About the cat, I mean.' He shook his head vigorously and a cloud of soot flew out. 'I'll tell my mother-in-law where it is; it's her responsibility. Maybe we ought to phone the fire brigade.'

This proved to be unnecessary; only moments after he had got back to Shingle Drive there was a knock on the door. It was the woman from Harbour Crescent; Biscuit had climbed down just after Mr Hooper had left, and run out of the house. Mr Hooper had still been in sight at the corner of the road. She was most apologetic that she'd been unable to catch hold of it, but it really was a rather wild brute.

Grandma was inconsolable, but Mr Hooper was able to laugh about it, later, when he'd washed his face and hair, and had something to eat. What a ridiculous incident! Squinting up a chimney, shouting 'Biscuit!' in a strange woman's house, and getting covered in soot!

'I shouldn't laugh too much,' Beth said.

'Why not?'

'I think we ought to stay here tonight.'

'What!'

'It's Sunday tomorrow. We don't have to go home; Kim's not there. Mother's so upset I think it would only be nice to stay.'

'Oh no. No!'

'I've made up my mind, Cliff. And the cat's still missing. We *must* find him!'

Mr Hooper groaned.

They made their way to Neil's sister's flat in Camden Town. A bedroom, a lounge, a kitchen and a bathroom, one floor of a crumbling old Victorian house: it seemed a palace after the hovel in Notting Hill Gate. Wendy was twenty; she worked for an estate agent. Very attractive, Kim thought, as he watched her padding about the kitchen, preparing a meal for them, with her shoulder-length blonde hair and tight trousers that made her move most agreeably. He wondered how she managed to afford the rent on such a flat. 'You're wasting your time, the pair of you,' she said, as they recounted the day's exploits. 'Is she worth it, this girl?' The question was directed at Kim, but she didn't want an answer, for she added, shaking boiled rice vigorously in a sieve, 'You could find yourself a dozen nicer girls.'

'What about me?' Neil asked.

'You have to take what you can get, big brother,' she said rudely, then turned and flashed a smile at Kim. Interesting, he thought. Maybe she fancies me.

'If you could help us it would save a lot of time,' Neil said, yawning. 'I'm worn out.'

'I'm far too busy.'

'What shall we do this evening? Do we continue?'

Kim mentioned the possibility of Soho. 'You can hardly expect me to go there,' Wendy said. 'Anyway, I'm going out with David.' So she has a boy-friend, Kim realized, and was surprised that he felt a pang of disappointment.

It was a remarkable situation, he reflected during the meal, quite bizarre. Here he was in a part of London he had not visited before, in a strange flat, chatting amicably with a girl he had never heard of yesterday, and her brother, whom, twenty-four hours ago, he had never spoken to, whom he had regarded as his worst enemy, someone he could easily murder. In the pub last night he had rapidly decided that Neil's feelings of anguish about Judith were totally genuine; not only that, he was pleasant and interesting himself. Only the first few minutes had been difficult; they had been like two dogs sniffing each other. Neil, more than Kim, wanted to make friends. It was as if the company of someone who had also been Judith's boy-friend was some kind of solace to him, a way of making her seem less distant, even if that boy was only an inexperienced youth not quite eighteen. Kim responded. They discussed Judith and almost nothing else. They had both formed exactly the same impression of her; it differed in no way. Kim was interested to learn that Neil had known her for a long time, had been with her on and off all last year : it had never come to much because she kept finding other men more willing to spend their money.

Last night Kim had slept soundly for the first time in three weeks. And now, while he chatted with Neil and Wendy, discovering that all three of them liked playing tennis, that all three of them hated the taste of rum, and Judith was for a moment forgotten, he found he was enjoying himself. When he realized this he was surprised. Perhaps the mind and the feelings could take so much and no more; was this the beginning of the cure? Was he still in love with Judith? Yes, for she produced the same reaction in him, the sinking sensation in the pit of the stomach, part pleasant, part a faint nausea, and his head whirled with all the unanswered questions about what had happened to her. If only he could find her, take her in his arms, sweep her off to some far distant place that was their own ... like a bridge over troubled water I will ease your mind ...

'I'll try the park by the Embankment,' Neil said. 'And some of the stations, Victoria, Charing Cross. What about you? Are you going to Soho?'

'Yes. All right.' He wasn't very keen on the idea.

'You watch it,' Wendy said.

Kim smiled. 'I haven't the money, and, even if I had, I don't think it's something I'd want to pay for.'

'I must change,' she said, looking at the clock. 'David will be here any minute. I hope you two will do the dishes before you go out.'

'She's all right,' Neil said, as he ran hot water into the sink. 'A bit sharp-tongued sometimes.'

'It must be nice having a sister. I'm an only child.'

'We only got really friendly when we grew up. A sort of alliance against our parents. They're a bit old-fashioned, I suppose. I don't mean we couldn't care less about them or anything like that. We often go home, but, well, they're not so easy to live with when you want to lead your own life.'

When they had finished the washing-up Neil rang Judith's mother. He had promised to do so at least once a day while they were in London. She had no news for them; Judith had not returned, written or phoned.

'It's as if everybody's waiting, listening for a word,' Kim said. 'But there's only silence.'

FOUR

He wished Neil was with him: it seemed very unsafe, loitering in Compton Street and Greek Street, watching women in doorways, and having his questions overheard by unsavoury-looking bystanders. When the women discovered that he didn't want to go inside for what they called 'a nice sexy time' they immediately lost interest, some telling him to beat it and stop pestering them, others glancing so quickly at the photograph before shaking their heads that they could not possibly have known whether they recognized Judith or not. As he walked on Kim thought it less likely than ever that Judith had come to London for such a purpose; these women were of a quite different nature from her. Almost without exception they revolted him, with their dyed hair, their cheap make-up, their evident hostility towards anyone who wasn't immediately going to pay for what they had to offer. Only one young thing, a mousy little girl with a voice so quiet he could hardly hear what she said, seemed to him to come in any way near to being pleasant, and his reaction to her, he guessed, was not because she was sexually attractive but because he felt sorry for her. She looked miserably unhappy. New to the game, he decided. She was the only one who gave Judith's picture any real attention; no, she said, there was no-one at all like that round here.

Kim gave up. He walked towards Shaftesbury Avenue to buy himself a coffee, but found he was stopping from time to time outside the strip clubs, his attention held by the photographs. It might be a possibility, he thought, and he rang some of the doorbells. No, no, she didn't work here was the inevitable response; try so-and-so further down the street. Why did the girls follow this sort of life, he wondered; what drove them to prostitution, or taking their clothes off several times a night in front of an audience of dirty old men? Or young men, come to that; he recognized in himself the same lust, the desire to see, the same excitement he experienced when he was waiting at the barber's, flicking through the pages of Penthouse or Playboy. You never read the articles, just looked at the pictures. Sex objects, receptacles for men, not real women; and these flesh and blood women here turned themselves into that: did they retain, deep inside themselves, some integrity? For the prostitutes the money was probably good: but nowadays it seemed odd. Poverty would hardly be the driving force, not like in the last century, and, in any case, there surely wasn't the same need for it as there used to be. Most people accepted that sex outside marriage was no longer forbidden; why give money for what could be found, quite easily, without paying? Because, he reflected, sex meant a relationship on some level or another, and the men who came here could not be bothered with that, or perhaps were incapable of it. As for the women, he was unable to fathom their cast of mind. He had read somewhere that prostitutes despised men: sex, to them, was possible with several different men every night because it in no way turned them on; it was meaningless, without pleasure, just an easy lazy way of earning money. It was difficult to imagine how the feelings could be so damaged that that was the result.

Yet hadn't Judith's feelings been irrevocably damaged by her upbringing? Not like that, of course, but maimed, nevertheless. And his own: being in love hadn't brought him much happiness; sex had not made the stars dance. But no, the comparison was absurd. Even if growing up involved some kind of tarnishing, a wounding of the self, nothing had crippled him.

He showed Judith's photograph to the man behind the counter in the coffee bar, but without success. After he had finished his drink he tried a few other restaurants and cafés around Leicester Square and St Martin's Lane, then, on the spur of the moment, he decided to go back to the flat. It was all quite futile, a complete waste of time. Why was he doing it anyway? Suppose he did find Judith. There was no reason to think she would return home. He couldn't force her. The police, perhaps, might be able to do so; she was not yet eighteen. But if she went under duress, she would only run away again, and, in a few months' time, she would be an adult and free to live whatever life she chose. There were, of course, other considerations. If he found her he would know, and so would Neil and her mother, where she was; some contact would have been made, however tenuous. They would know she was alive; that would at least be something.

But what is there for me, Kim wondered. No chance of their relationship being resumed, on any terms. Just an aching void. It was time for another girl. But he didn't want another girl, had no intention of looking.

What a terrible place London is, he thought, as he walked down the escalator at Tottenham Court Road into the warm used air pushed backwards and forwards by the tube trains. The air above ground was different, but equally unpleasant with its acrid petrol fumes. The constant noise of traffic slowing and accelerating, the crowds of people hurrying everywhere, the dirt, the scraps of paper blown about the streets, the grimy unwashed windows, the dog shit, the filth in every paving-stone crevice, the lies of advertisement hoardings, the graffiti— 'West Ham Boot Boys Rule, O.K.', 'Vote National Front', 'Chelsea power'— the sexual exploitation: those men in the amusement arcades, the women in the Soho doorways, the pictures outside the clubs and cinemas. And why were contraceptive machines hidden away in public lavatories, as if they were sordid things and a stripper or a tart was not? And these kids run away from home because they imagine London means excitement, real life, adulthood! As absurd as thinking the streets of the city were paved with gold.

He thought of his own home, his room, his parents. He had been exceptionally trying to Mum and Dad recently. He made a resolution to spend more time with them, work harder at school, go out with his friends on Fridays and Saturdays, take one of the girls to a disco. Then he wondered how long the resolution would last, or if he would act on it at all.

He was surprised to find Wendy in, ironing some clothes. 'You're back early,' she said.

'Yes. I got fed up.'

'Thought you might.'

'I didn't expect to see you, either.'

'We had a row,' she said crossly, and slithered the iron with great energy over a sheet. 'Neil's not home yet. He'll stick it out longer than you.'

'What do you mean?'

'He's got less sense.' Kim did not know how to answer that. 'He never has with girls, and this Judith seems to have driven him demented. And her on hard drugs.' She folded up the sheet. 'Are you into any of that sort of thing?'

'Me? No way. Never even smoked pot.'

'Good. I've seen what it can do to you.'

'Marijuana's not addictive, they say.'

'Maybe it isn't. Maybe it's quite harmless. But have you ever seen a room full of people who are stoned out of their tiny minds? Well, I have, more than once. Nothing could be more *boring*. All these kids lying about each in their private ecstasies. No communication. No fun. A cheap short cut in my opinion, like wanking, a sort of second-rate substitute. What are you laughing at?'

'You. You're very aggressive. And I don't think I've heard a girl say wank before.'

'It's an ugly word.' She switched off the iron. 'I'm not aggressive, not really. It's just this whole Judith thing annoys me intensely. What a *drag!* Let her get on with it, I say. It won't do Neil any good even if he does find her.'

'I was thinking the same. As far as I'm concerned.'

'Were you!' She looked at him. 'Well, that's an advance, certainly.' She picked up her purse and counted her money. 'Let's go out for a drink.'

'Now that sounds the most sensible idea I've heard all day.'

'God! I need one. We had a row; I told you. Finito. For good.' She smiled. 'I'm more annoyed than sorry.'

They went to the Mitre, a pleasant Victorian pub, full of shiny wood and lots of mirrors. It was crowded and noisy; someone was playing all the old songs on an out-of-tune piano, and most of the customers joined in with the words: *Daisy, Daisy; My Old Man's a Dustman* : typical London Saturday night. Wendy knew the place, and found a quiet corner. They drank slowly, a couple of pints each in an hour. She surprised him again; he'd never been out with a girl who drank pints of beer. And they talked. It was easy and relaxed; he listened to Wendy chatting about her job, how she loved London and hated it at the same time, about her mother who was a bit of a snob and a dreadful old fusspot and, even worse, the secretary of the local bridge club. Kim told her that he was not very close to his parents either; then they discussed the history of his feelings for Judith, his school, his hopes for university entrance.

I'd like to sleep with her, he thought, then found himself mildly shocked at the idea. A girl of twenty, thoroughly sophisticated, and he, a fumbling schoolboy not yet eighteen! Absurd! Judith. It was the first time for many months that he'd contemplated any girl in that way, apart from her. Sleep with her, he said to himself; look how he'd phrased it: that was indicative. Just sex. Always, ever since that time when he was fourteen and he'd fallen in love with Judith, he'd considered sex and love as matters that should be inseparable; he'd never really wanted to go to bed with anybody other than Judith, and then only if she loved him too. Look what had happened! Anna had been the only sexual experience, and he hadn't loved her. Would it ever come right? If he and Wendy did, and they wouldn't he was certain, even if he'd guessed correctly that she found him attractive, it wouldn't make for happiness any more than with the other two. How much better was it than the sordidness he had seen today, the boy who'd approached him, the prostitutes, the strip-club photographs? Hardly sordid like that of course, but... well... it would be just as selfish. Shouldn't love-making be a giving as well as a taking? A giving of the self, of the emotions, a commitment. Yes, that was it: a commitment, on both sides, equally, the ultimate step that showed you both meant something very important to each other.

'You haven't been listening to a single word,' said Wendy, severely. 'What have I just asked you?'

'I don't know.' He laughed, nervously.

'Thinking about Judith, I suppose.'

'No. Not at all.'

'What, then?'

'You, if you must know.' He felt himself blushing, and wished he hadn't said that.

'Oh!' She looked very interested. 'What, exactly?'

'I couldn't possibly tell you! Not now.'

'Oh, I see!' She stood up. 'Let's go. They've already called time.' On the way back she said 'I was talking about Neil. I asked what you thought of him.'

'Neil... it's strange. I was so jealous of him. I could have killed him. I really could! Now that's all gone. It's just simply... vanished. Thank Christ! It's vile, jealousy. Loathsome and degrading. It does the most dreadful things to you, warps everything out of perspective.'

'And now?'

'I like him. I mean I really like him. I'd like to know him, not just to be linked because of Judith. And... it's odd... I feel sorry for him.'

'Sorry for him?'

'Yes. The whole business with Judith. I think I'm getting it into proportion. I mean, I don't know how long I'm going to go on with this searching everywhere. If I get fed up I'll go home in a day or two. And he, I don't think he'll give up. At least not so quickly as me.'

'And you're still in love with Judith?'

'Yes. Certainly.'

'Well, I'm not so sure that you are.' She dug around in her bag for the front-door key, found it, dropped it, picked it up and dropped it again. They both reached down for it, banged their heads together, then eventually got inside, giggling wildly. Neil was in the kitchen, frowning. He seemed to disapprove of his sister and Kim enjoying themselves when there were more serious matters to consider.

'We only went out for a quick drink,' Wendy said, defensively.

Neil's day had been a waste of time. Even had a rude exchange with a policeman, who seemed to think he was soliciting. He was dog tired; *he* hadn't stopped for a glass of beer. He was going to bed, and no, in answer to a question from Wendy, he didn't want a bath now. He'd probably fall asleep and drown himself. Tomorrow they could continue the search; there were a number of new possibilities he'd thought of: they could discuss them in the morning. He went off into the lounge. He and Kim were to sleep on the sofa; it turned into a double bed.

'Do you want a bath?' Wendy asked.

'I'd love one.'

Kim lay in the hot water for a long time, his body pleasantly drowsy, his mind spinning with apparent irreconcilables. I want to sleep with her. But I love Judith. I don't love Judith as much as I did. Perhaps I don't love her at all. I want to sleep with Wendy, more than when I first thought I did. Of course I love Judith. It was all uneasy, uncertain: when he and Neil had talked about the idea of coming to London to look for her—it was only yesterday—he had felt, in a way he hadn't for weeks, months, really good: the jealousy was fading, the moping about finished. There was the prospect of doing something positive and worthwhile; he'd felt clean. Moral, perhaps, was a better word. Now, for quite different reasons, he didn't like himself again; he was being selfish and immoral.

He came out of the bathroom dressed only in a towel; Wendy had probably gone to bed. But there was a light under the kitchen door: he had better say goodnight.

'I've made you a cup of tea,' she said. He went in, apologizing for the towel. 'Good Lord, you don't think I'm embarrassed that easily, do you?' she scoffed.

They talked about music; Wendy, too, liked Simon and Garfunkel, had the same record. When he had finished his tea Kim stood up. 'Goodnight,' he said, not wanting to leave. He wanted to kiss her. She stood up too, put the cups in the sink. He moved towards her, hesitated, then put his arms round her. It will be dreadful if the towel falls off, he thought as they kissed.

She followed him, and they kissed again in the hallway. He turned to open the lounge door. He could hear Neil snoring. 'Don't go in there,' she said, stroking his bare arm.

He was silent, his heart almost missing a beat. 'I must,' he said.

'Why?'

'It's very complicated. Don't think I don't want to.' He smiled. 'That's what I was daydreaming about in the pub.'

'I know.'

'It's all very complicated,' he repeated, lamely.

She looked at him a moment, then went into the bedroom. He was now thoroughly aroused, shaking with excitement. The selfishness, the immorality, seemed unsure concepts, dissolving like sandcastles. What was there to gain from refusal? He recalled what she'd said about masturbation, for that, now, was the only alternative. He wanted her. Oh, why the hell not, he thought; he'd regret it for ever if he didn't. He went into her bedroom.

He would be perfectly happy if he was at home doing nothing, but here he was bored. Grandma's sitting-room made it so intolerable: the plastic ducks on the wall, the grinning pixies bought in cheap souvenir shops at seaside resorts in the West Country, the statuette of a little girl, nineteen twenties style, coyly holding the hem of her skirt and masquerading as a table lamp. The old lady resolutely refused to be cheered up about the loss of her cat, though Beth did her utmost; Biscuit would be yowling for food outside the back door in the morning, she said several times. 'No he won't,' Grandma replied. 'He's run over. I know he is. Dead in a ditch somewhere.' And she dabbed at her eyes.

Later they played Scrabble. It was a game Mr Hooper liked, though it annoyed him when he lost. He usually felt he should win when he surveyed the opposition, particularly if the forces ranged against him consisted of his wife and his mother-in-law. He did the Telegraph crossword puzzle every day, and thought that he had a greater fluency with words than either of the two women. Once in a while he could finish the crossword in ten minutes. But fate was not often on his side in Scrabble; he could see the connections, knew where to score the highest points, but there was always a letter missing, or he had too many consonants, or got stuck with the Q when there was no U available. Tonight the game went as it frequently did, Grandma way ahead, having most of the luck. Then he suddenly saw a possibility of doing something he had never been able to do before: getting rid of all his letters. He had two Ns, O, G, A, T and I. There was a G with nothing beside it. He put the letters on the board: TANGOING. It was a triple score with the first G, and by adding on the points for going out with all seven letters, he was an easy winner.

'What's that?' Grandma asked, peering at the board.

'Present participle of the verb "to tango".'

'No such word.'

'Yes, there is.'

'It's the name of a dance. You can't talk about tangoing.'

'Why not? You can talk about waltzing. Why not tangoing? You can probably even have chachachaing.'

'Tango's Spanish, so it isn't allowed.'

'Look it up in the dictionary, then.'

She did so. Tango was acceptable, as a noun or a verb. She went out to the toilet, full of grumbles.

'You might have let her win,' Beth said.

'Why?'

'Tonight of all nights, when she's so upset.'

'That's absurd! If you don't play with some hope of winning, you might as well not play at all! Anyway, she always wins. Somebody else's turn to do so.'

Beth looked annoyed. 'You're like a child,' she said.

' I'm not.'

She patted the cushions, tidied up the sofa. 'Wind's getting up.'

'Yes. It is.'

It was beginning to blow in strongly off the sea. It suited his mood; he would have liked a real gale. I'll huff and I'll puff and I'll blow your house down. He was surprised at himself. He wasn't a destructive person, never wished other people any harm. Why was he feeling so violent? He was puzzled, and it bothered him that he couldn't fathom the reason. If gigantic waves were crashing over the top of the pebble ridge by morning it would be an awesome sight. They wouldn't be, of course. The ridge curbed the power of the sea. It had been reinforced with concrete blocks at the back; danger was kept at bay: it was safe, but somehow dull. And he would be horrified, naturally, if the water did pour in and flood the houses, drowning people, making them lose their possessions. But ... what was this but? He didn't know.

Grandma returned. What was Kim doing, she wondered. This was her other theme of the evening; she didn't once say outright that she considered her grandson thoughtless and unkind for not coming to visit her, but she hinted at it constantly. He was growing up so fast, and she saw so little of him; there wouldn't perhaps be that many more occasions to enjoy his company before she passed on: when she was a girl, the young lived near the old, not like today when they all moved to new housing estates as soon as they got married, and their elderly relatives were shunted down to colonies for the aged at the seaside, Bognor, Pevensey, Peacehaven. It was her own choice, Mr

Hooper thought; she could have stayed near us, in the house at Coulsdon.

'They live so much for the present nowadays,' she went on. 'All the latest crazes, clothes, pop music. Last year's fashions forgotten the minute this year's are in. They've no time for the past.'

'They have their own lives to lead,' Mr Hooper said.

'That's just it! No sense of family any more.'

'That's not necessarily true. And families can be very restricting to young people.'

'This one isn't,' Beth said, sharply. 'We've always let Kim do what he wanted. Within reason. I agree with Mother. He could have gone up to London another time, when we weren't doing anything special.'

'London!' Grandma sniffed. 'Two lads on the loose. Up to no good, I'll be bound.'

'That's exactly what young people object to,' Mr Hooper said. 'Us imagining every time they want to be on their own that they're up to no good. Kim isn't like that. I can't think there's a great deal he'd be doing that we wouldn't approve of. Isn't that so, Beth?'

'Yes. On the whole.'

'I'm not saying he isn't a good boy,' Grandma said. 'He *is* a good boy. One of the best.'

'What are we arguing about then?'

'Oh, I don't know.' She looked tired and old. 'But I wish I knew what had happened to that cat. Do either of you want a cup of tea before we go to bed?'

'I'll make it.' Mr Hooper went out to the kitchen, glad to be busy. Beth joined him a moment later.

'Lay off it, Cliff, will you!'
'What?'
'Mother.'
'Yes. I'm sorry.' He was. She was a poor old woman at the fag-end of her life, lonely, disappointed and bored, with nothing much left to live for. Thinking of Kim, himself, and her, he wondered if it always had to be a lengthy downhill journey. Not necessarily, of course, but that often seemed to be the pattern. It wasn't true for his grandparents. They had been born in the horse and buggy age and lived to see jet aeroplanes and plastic, but they had not died lost lonely souls. At sixty-eight his grandmother had taken a long holiday in Paris, to revisit the scenes of her youth, and she had thoroughly enjoyed herself. As a teenage girl she'd worked as a nursemaid for a family attached to the British Embassy, and once she'd woken up at four in the morning to get herself a good viewpoint for the military ceremony when Dreyfus had his epaulettes struck off. In her seventies she'd taken up gardening and won prizes for her flowers and vegetables, year after year; she was picking grapes from her own vine when she fell down dead from a heart attack. A very impressive person she was.

Beth's mother was right about one thing, though: Bognor, Pevensey, Peacehaven; they were dreadful mistakes, particularly if you were like her, with no interest in life except the cat and the occasional family visit. He had a horrible vision of himself ending up the same way, for he suffered from a similar fault: not a lack of interest in life, but there was nothing in which he could totally absorb himself outside Beth, Kim, the garden and the house. They suddenly seemed fragile and fallible, particularly Kim. He would have to do something, he decided, before it was too late. The question was, what?

FIVE

'What was all that about it being so complicated, then?'

He was lying on his back, staring at the ceiling. 'It wasn't.'

'I didn't think so either.'

'Oh?' He looked at her. 'It was all right?'

She laughed. 'Why do you need your ego boosted?'

'Do I?'

'Yes.'

She was beautiful. He wished he was older, more sure of things. 'It doesn't seem at all complicated now,' he said. 'I just have this feeling... well, maybe I'm naïve. Leaping into bed with someone you hardly know, even if you want to a lot... I think, I always thought anyway, that sex... it's a commitment, a sign of something long-term, only good if you're both in love. Perhaps that's just an adolescent fantasy.'

'No. No, I don't think so. Anyway we do know each other... it's happened quite quickly. Much more quickly than usual, yes. I wouldn't make love with someone I didn't trust, however gorgeous.'

'But how can you be sure that you trust me? And what do you mean trust?'

'I don't *know*. Not for sure. But I think so.'

'I don't understand.'

'It isn't merely strong arms, or attractive hair, or honest eyes, even though you've got all those. It's some intuition about... the possibility of a relationship with someone, isn't it? More than they're just interesting. Some inkling of... I can't find any other word than trust.'

'But I have to go home in a day or two and that might be the end of it. How do you know it won't?'

'I don't, do I? Of course you've got to go home, but I hope I'll see you again, very soon.'

'Is it... is it anything to do with the row you had with David?'

'David! No!'

'It's just that this... this implies a commitment, if we're not to regret it. And Judith... she seems to be slipping away incredibly fast, and I don't like myself for letting that happen. Sex ought to come when there's commitment.'

'You do keep using that word! In this case sex came first, and I don't see why it should mean at a later date we shouldn't be committed... it sounds like going to jail!' She giggled. 'Do not pass go. Do not collect two hundred pounds.' She turned over. 'It doesn't make that amount of difference, Kim.'

'Maybe. But I feel I've cheated.'

'Oh, you're impossible!'

'I'm sorry. I didn't mean to spoil it.'

'You haven't.' They were silent for some time. 'Look, Kim, I'm not going to say I love you, because I can't begin to know yet, and I can't say we ought to rush out and get married just because we've been to bed together—'

'Married! Christ!'

'Well there you are, then.'

'That's what I don't know. Where I am.'

'You think too much.'

'Do I?'

'You seem to me to be a rather physical person.'

'What? Just now?'

'I meant generally. The way you move. Like a games player.'

'Well, I am. I like charging about the football field. Doesn't mean I have to be a moron, though.'

'I didn't mean that. I thought, someone with mind and body in harmony. When things are not going badly.'

'They are going badly.'

'Thanks very much!'

'I'm sorry. That wasn't meant. No, you're right. I do think too much. Why don't I just enjoy myself?'

'You're...' But her words were lost as he put his arms round her and kissed her.

He was woken by the sound of Neil banging about in the kitchen, but he felt too lazy to move. Wendy lay beside him, asleep. The first time he'd ever spent a night in bed with a girl: that was tender and marvellous, her warm body curled again his; that was trust. Her smooth limbs touching his rough, hairy skin. He thawed inside:

happiness. He was more certain now that something could come of this, something that could last. But there was a lot to learn. Even sharing a bed was not easy; he had lain against her all night, one arm round her, one knee between her legs, and now his back ached, and he had slept badly, waking often because he was so hot.

The one thing he didn't want to do was to spend the day searching for Judith. He would much rather have the time alone with Wendy. A day together, seeing the sights of London, going out for a meal, dancing, coming home to share the bed again. He laughed at his inconsistency: London suddenly seemed to have beautiful and romantic qualities; it wasn't all dirt and grime, sordid sex, squalid houses, unwashed hippies. The two of them at St. Paul's or the Tower or the Tate Gallery, or walking hand in hand in the park in the autumn sunlight, feet crunching the fallen leaves. Yes, he thought as he put his clothes on, you make judgements about somewhere according to your own frame of mind, whether the experiences you have there are nice or nasty; it's nothing to do with the place itself: ugliness is in the eye of the beholder, like beauty. The place has neither, usually.

But it wouldn't be possible to spend the day alone with her. It would be most unfair to Neil, even though Neil was now looking at him across the kitchen table in a rather antagonistic way. It wasn't, he imagined, because he'd made love with Wendy; it was probably that Neil didn't like the fact of his sleeping with anybody, as if it meant a betrayal of Judith. Neil suggested the railway stations, Charing Cross, Victoria, London Bridge. He hadn't had time last night to visit them. She could have arrived at any one of those three; somebody there might have seen her.

'But it's Sunday,' Kim objected. 'There'll be hardly anyone there. Skeleton staff.'

'I think it's worth trying,' Neil answered, with the kind of heavy patience one might use on a recalcitrant child. 'There'll be porters on duty, and people in the refreshment rooms and bars. And then we could go to the King's Road.'

'Saturday afternoon would have been best. All the freaks come out then.'

'We'll try it nevertheless. And Earl's Court, Notting Hill Gate, North Kensington. You only went to one house, but those districts are full of down-and-outs.'

'It's enough work for a week,' Kim grumbled.

'Don't you want to go on then?'

'I'll give it another day.'

'Another day! I thought you said you could stop till Tuesday.'

'Well . . . I think we're wasting our time.'

Neil shrugged his shoulders. 'I understand. Don't let me keep you from your new-found pleasures.'

Kim sighed. 'Come on. Let's get on with it.'

'Is Wendy up?'

'She should be by now. I'll take her a cup of tea.' She was curled up in the same position as when he had left the room, but her eyes were open.

'Another Judith hunt?' He nodded. 'You'd be better off staying here.'

He laughed. 'I'm sure I would! But I mustn't. And tomorrow you're working, I suppose.'

'As a matter of fact I'm not. I always have Monday off as I work Saturdays.'

His face lit up. 'That's great! We'll go out for the day, just the two of us. Shall we? Would you like that?'

'Yes, I would. Where to?'

'I don't mind. You choose. No Judith hunt tomorrow, I promise.'

The prospect of this was enough for Kim to feel that he could get through the day without being too much bothered by Neil's moroseness. They decided to work together; yesterday's effort, they both admitted, had seemed all the more depressing because they were alone. But the stations proved useless; they were almost deserted, and no-one to whom they showed the photograph recognized Judith. Everything had been planned wrongly, Kim thought, even though they had discussed what to do beforehand in some detail. Late at night was best for the stations, not Sunday morning, and Saturday for Earl's Court and Chelsea; then any time in the evenings would do for parks and benches. But Neil had a restless urge to be doing something, however futile. And he would himself, he knew, if it hadn't been for Wendy. She had altered him. He wasn't so much in love with Judith, not nearly so much. It was easier now to think of Judith as selfish, corrupt, not worth bothering about. Perhaps it was just a question of filling one's life with some absorbing new interest; Wendy was certainly that. When he had nothing, Judith filled his thoughts and occupied his feelings entirely.

Perhaps the jealousy had helped to destroy her, had burned out the obsession. Whatever it was, he was beginning to sense the delights of freedom, as if a dead weight that had hampered him for years was being lifted away.

Lunch-time saw them in a busy café in Chelsea. They ate ham sandwiches and drank coffee, watching the other customers, listening to conversations.

Neil said, staring hard into his half-finished cup, 'Don't raise your expectations too high with Wendy. You could end up the same way as I have with Judith.'

'What do you mean?'

'I'm talking about David.'

'What about him?' Kim felt suddenly tense, as if his hopes and daydreams were about to be smashed again.

'He's twenty-five. Works for a construction company. A very pleasant person, in fact. He and Wendy have been together for over a year, on and off. I say on and off, because they're both very quick-tempered people, too alike, too bloody dogmatic. They have great rows, never going to see each other again, then a fortnight later they've made it up. He's lived in the flat with her, pays half the rent.' That would explain a few oddities, Kim thought; the double bed, the Wella for Men and Denim on the dressing-table, a man's hair-brush. How she could afford such a place. 'He's not there at the moment because he's working in Chelmsford, has been for about six weeks. They'll be back together soon, I don't doubt.' Kim said nothing. Neil looked at him. 'I'm sorry. It's best you should know.'

Pride as well as hurt kept him silent, but eventually he

could not contain himself. He wanted to brush it off lightly, say it didn't matter a bit; a few nights in bed with an attractive girl were better than a few nights alone. But he couldn't. 'So I'm just a little bit of extra!' he said, bitterly. 'Probably just for the intention of making David jealous!'

'Why, what does she mean to you?'

'Nothing now.'

'Oh, come on! What did you expect? Whatever did you want?'

'I don't know. I did hope, though, for something more than a good screw.'

'I might be wrong. Maybe she has finished with him.'

'Does she always let the first man that comes along screw her when she's quarrelled with David?'

'Kim! She's not like that. I shouldn't think it's ever happened before.' He did not answer. 'Kim, didn't you wonder about him? You've got a lot to learn.' Neil's words were gentle, without malice.

'Yes. I have.'

The afternoon and early evening dragged by. They spoke to people in the King's Road and the streets round about, then took the District Line to Notting Hill Gate. Here there was some encouragement: artists were selling paintings and pottery on the Hyde Park side of the Bayswater Road, and many of the passing crowd seemed just the right types. But nothing, no clues. They ended up at Speaker's Corner, mingling with those who were listening to the maniacs and eccentrics shouting their wares, a health food fanatic, a man outraged by the thought that the government was in the pay of Soviet Russia, an antivivisectionist quoting bizarre facts and figures, a thuglike creature who wanted to have all the Blacks repatriated. No-one here had seen or heard of Judith. Kim tried to forget the new heart-ache but it wouldn't go away: it was almost pleasurable thinking the worst, revelling in self-pity. It was yet another negative emotion, he tried to tell himself, but it was so easy to indulge in. Was Wendy, at this moment, in bed with somebody else? Was she a nymphomaniac? Ridiculous. Neil had said that there weren't any other men. None that he knew of. How many were there that Wendy hadn't mentioned? Was there any hope? Yes, but more slender than he had thought. Hope for what? Did it really matter if she went back to David? He had spent a whole night with a girl. Wasn't that important in itself? There were millions of other girls. Millions. One, somewhere surely, he could fall in love with, who could fall in love with him. But dejection engulfed him like a fog. He was just an inexperienced seventeen-year-old. She'd just wanted a bloke to have sex with; anyone would do, who had—what did she say?—strong arms and honest eyes. Honest eyes! Naïve eyes. But she didn't mean that. She probably meant a bloke who looked as if he'd give her what she wanted. She'd also said something about trust, but self-pity drove it out of his head. Well, if she was after another good screw, he'd oblige. Get what you can, boy; might as well. Otherwise you'll have nothing. He wasn't going to get involved.

They went home. 'Why do you go on with it?' Kim

asked, when Neil began to outline plans for the following day.

'I don't know. I've wondered myself.'

'How much longer?'

'I go back to work on Tuesday.'

'Is it some sort of guilt you need to expiate?'

Neil frowned. 'I don't know. Maybe. I love her, that's all.'

'Yes.'

'And now you don't feel the same about her; well, that's all right for you, but it hasn't happened to me. Maybe it will. I know Judith isn't worth it and all that; yes, she probably deserves all she gets. But . . . there's nothing else, is there?'

He came to a decision. 'Neil, I might go home tomorrow.'

'That's up to you. You don't have to feel bound to go on looking just because of me. I'm grateful for your help. Honestly. But there's no need to stay if you don't want to.'

'Thanks. I may not go home. It depends . . . on Wendy.'

'I guessed so.'

'I may go out with her all day tomorrow. I don't know yet. Do you . . . do you mind?'

'You do what you like.'

'Thanks.'

'And don't keep saying thanks.'

Dinner was ready when they reached the flat, roast beef and Yorkshire pudding, a cherry pie. Wendy was an excellent cook. 'Which of you two boys is taking me out tonight?' she asked.

'Not me,' Neil said. 'I'm shattered. I shall have a bath, watch telly, and go to bed early.'

'I'm shattered too,' said Kim. 'Corns and smelly feet, aching legs. All that walking.'

'Oh.'

'I'll take you out, though. Don't you worry yourself.'

She sensed his coolness, and looked at him quizzically, raising one eyebrow.

Mr Hooper found it impossible to sleep although he was back in his own house. Staying at Pevensey in an unfamiliar bed seemed to have broken the rhythm of his nights. He listened to Beth's even breathing, and shifted a little, trying to make himself comfortable. But he was less comfortable now than he had been before; in ten minutes' time he would have pins and needles in his left arm. He wanted to roll right over and find a completely different position, but that would disturb Beth. He freed his arm, and lay on his back. Now there was a pain between his shoulder-blades. He stared at the ceiling for some while, hoping the pain would go away if he didn't think about it. It was worse. Cancer? Ridiculous. No use, no use at all, he thought. He slipped quietly out of bed, made his way across the room and went downstairs.

He found the sleeping pills in the kitchen cupboard—Beth had them on prescription, for she, too, suffered about once a month from a night of insomnia—and he swallowed one with a glass of water. He made himself a cup of tea and stared blankly at the dying embers of the lounge fire. The pill didn't seem to be working, then he remembered it usually took about half an hour to make him feel drowsy. He picked up the Daily Telegraph, but he'd read it all earlier. *Mrs Thatcher flays Prime Minister,* screamed the headline. Same old depressing stuff. He had a vision of the Iron Lady beating Jim Callaghan black and blue with a cat-o'-nine-tails, and thought how absurd it was, the way journalists wrote up the news. *New shock for Foot. Socialists on brink of defeat. Strikers hold Callaghan to ransom.* Labour governments, according to the papers, were invariably on the point of being electrocuted, drowned, kidnapped, or thrashed: it was a wonder they survived at all.

No point in sitting down here. He went upstairs slowly, hoping the pill would take its effect as soon as he got into bed. Kim's door was open. He looked in. All neat and clean as the boy was away; Beth had been tidying up. The desk where Kim worked: table-lamp, chemistry books, files, paper. He glanced through one of the files. Meaningless hieroglyphics; formulae, diagrams labelled X, Y and Z. Something to do with the manufacture of chlorine in Kim's typically unreadable handwriting. A small bookcase with a few dog-eared paperbacks. What did his son read these days? James Hadley Chase, Russell Braddon, Harold Robbins. Valley of the Dolls. The Moors Murderers. The Spy who Came in from the Cold. They hadn't been touched for a long time. He didn't often see Kim curled up with a book. The record-player. Focus, Deep Purple, Bread, Queen, Simon and Garfunkel. Not his taste. You could never hear the words properly in these modern songs.

He looked at the walls. A map of Dorset that had been there for years, a souvenir of a holiday when Kim was... what? Twelve? Thirteen? He couldn't remember. A poster of a negress, some singer or other he assumed. On the mantelpiece a candle, an ash-tray, and a half-empty packet of Embassy tipped. He opened the wardrobe. What am I doing, he asked himself. He wouldn't like it if he found Kim snooping in *his* personal property. That was it: personal. Areas, even in the people you lived with, your own son, that were private. Right that it should be so, of course, but sad too: as children grew up, more and more of their lives became separate, no admittance to the older generation, particularly parents. Tee-shirts, jeans, sweaters: any young man's clothes. Nothing distinctive about them. He realized that this was what he was searching for, something about Kim, a clue that he had not known was there. It wasn't in this room. This room had nothing unique, nothing that said Kim and no-one else. The private Kim was kept hidden.

He opened one of the drawers of the desk. It was quite wrong to do so, he knew; though he was Kim's father he had no more business here than a complete stranger. It was full of letters. One was postmarked Berlin. 'Hi Kim!' it said. 'Hope you're still raving it up in good old Purley! Apologies for not having written before now. I had intended writing as soon as I got to Germany, but I've been here ten days or more already and I'm still busy ploughing my way through the red tape and bureaucracy one encounters when enrolling at a foreign university. I feel certain I've filled up more than a hundred bloody forms already. Seriously, it's been a bind, (I haven't even had time to have a good drink yet—things must be bad!). We're living in a rather smooth flat overlooking the part of the city I live near, and much to my delight it has separate bathroom and kitchen, and a very large living room with a bed/settee in one corner. Make sure you drop me a few lines toute de suite, you lazy punk, and let me know how you are doing. I drove over here with Zoë on the 18/19th and the car stood up perfectly—that's Triumphs for you! Since then I've been lazing around waiting for term to start. The weather hasn't been too hot (it's bloody miserable) so there's been no sun-bathing, but we have managed to get out into the countryside around here once or twice. Write soon, won't you. Cheers, Steve.'

Who was Steve? Obviously someone a year or two older than Kim. Were all his friends older than he was? The ease with which young people sped around Europe! Berlin! Hitler's final days in the bunker, Allied bombs, then air-lifts, Stalin, the Cold War: that was what Berlin meant to him, and now English kids were enrolling at its university, driving over there in their cars, and frolicking in the countryside with girls called Zoë.

He replaced the letter and closed the drawer. He yawned. Sleep was coming at last. He was tempted to open another drawer; decided against it, then did so. A pile of magazines: *The Aeromodeller, The Young Scientist, Films and Filming.* At the bottom three copies of *Playboy.* He pulled one of them out and flicked through the pages. The women seemed as impersonal as this room.

Kim ogling at *Playboy!* But... why not? He'd gazed at the pictures in *Men Only* when he was seventeen. They were called 'ladies out of uniform', he remembered. But the thought of his son drooling over stuff like this made him once again feel old. He put it away carefully under *The Young Scientist.* Hidden down there, of course, in case he or Beth saw them. What would Beth say? She would hardly approve. Amusing, though: he'd done just that himself, years back, so *his* parents wouldn't find out.

'What are you doing?'

He jumped, feeling the same guilt he might have experienced if it had been his mother and not Beth standing in the doorway. Yes, the drawer was shut; nothing in the room looked as if he had been behaving like a burglar. 'I can't sleep,' he said. 'I've taken one of your pills.'

'But why did you come in here?' She yawned, and pulled her dressing-gown more tightly round her.

'No particular reason.'

She looked at him, bewildered. 'I woke up because you weren't there. I never do sleep for long without you.'

'Habit.'

'Yes.'

'I wouldn't like to sleep on my own. Not after all these years.'

'I should think not!'

'Kim does.'

'He's used to it.'

'One day...'

'One day what?'

'He won't. Sleep on his own.'

'Probably. What *are* you on about now?'

'Nothing. Old age.'

'Old age my foot! You're forty-three! The prime of life, and still as attractive as you ever were!'

'Where's it all gone?'

'In living. Come back to bed! It's hardly the time of night to start getting philosophical.'

'All right.' The bed was warm and he now felt very sleepy. 'Don't you wish, Beth, that sometimes you could begin all over again? Knowing what you know now?'

'No. Do you?'

'Maybe. Though one's a lot more certain of some things, I suppose. Who you are. What you can do and what you can't, and being content not to try what's impossible. All that falling in and out of love they go in for at their age! They do have a great capacity for not enjoying themselves, the young.'

'Hmmm. I think they enjoy themselves quite enough these days. Too much, sometimes.'

'You're jealous.'

'I'm not.'

'Yes, you are.'

'All right, I'm jealous! Do shut up and go to sleep, will you?' She turned over and yanked the bedclothes round her, determined to stop any further conversation.

'Goodnight, Beth.'

She muttered something inaudible. Waves of tiredness swept over him; when the pill was beginning to work it engulfed him so quickly, so pleasantly, almost like a surgeon taking him to pieces, picking out the unfunctioning parts and gently healing them. He thought of the sea, not the grey water of Pevensey, but the white Atlantic breakers of war-time childhood holidays in Devon; he was a little child again, utterly happy, racing across the yellow sand, into the huge dissolving sea.

SIX

Most of the evening was spent in heated arguments. Kim was surprised at himself. He had considered during the meal what sort of attitude he should adopt; distant and monosyllabic he had decided: in his mind he'd planned out bits of conversation in which he kept her guessing; she would be anxious and unhappy, and he would enjoy punishing her. It didn't work out like that at all. Wendy was not in any way anxious or unhappy; she attacked him vigorously, said he was childish and demanding, refused to accept reality, lived in a world of immature teenage fantasy. Kim fought back. That was what surprised him. He stood up to her, shouted at her: he'd never spoken like that to a girl before. She was a slut, a tart; she'd deceived and cheated him. 'I wanted a relationship!' he yelled, banging his fist on a table. 'Not a one-night stand! Not with you!'

'Be quiet! People are staring.' They were at a disco, and though the noise was deafeningly loud, heads were turned in their direction.

'I'd like to put you over my knee and slap you.'

'You'd enjoy that, I suppose.' She laughed.

'Are you going to see him again or not?'

'I'm certainly not going to be blackmailed by you. Or anybody else. I'm quite free to do what I like; I'm not tied down to anybody.'

'Give him up.'

'No. The more you say that, the more likely I'll go back to him.'

'So it was nothing more than a good shaft you wanted from me!'

'Kim, please . . . I want us! Just let's see if it happens, shall we?'

'I don't understand. He can offer you so much more than I can. I'm only a kid.'

'That's not the point.'

'What is the point, then?'

'Look. Listen. I don't intend to get in touch with David at all. Absolutely no intention, not this time, it's gone too far. He'll probably ring me up or come round, Tuesday or Wednesday. It may work out, I don't know. However I'm pretty certain it won't. Because of you, you fool! You weren't there the other times! No-one was. I hadn't met anybody else, not anybody I wanted, and now I have. I want to go on seeing you. Please.' She put her hand on his; he took it, held it gently.

'Will you go on seeing him?'

'I might. I might not.'

'And sleep with him?'

'I'm not promising anything.'

'No, you certainly aren't!'

'Kim, it's too *early* to promise anything!'

'All right. I give in.' He smiled. 'I always do. Come on, let's dance. It's "Rock your baby". George McCrae.'

But the quarrel flared up again several times, and fizzled out in the same way: Kim couldn't leave matters alone. She had been very patient with him, he thought as they walked home; perhaps he did mean something to her. It was the same when they were undressing, but when they were in bed, they were silent at last. 'Goodnight,' was all she murmured afterwards, as she shifted in his arms, making the pillow more comfortable, fitting herself round the shape of his body, and 'Mmm' was all he replied as he slipped towards sleep. He almost wanted to giggle he'd pushed the argument so hard, and not once had she got really fed up, not once told him she didn't want to see him again. The happiness he'd felt that morning was to some extent restored.

Over breakfast they made plans for the day, deciding to visit places in London they'd never been to before. Though both of them had lived most of their lives on the edges of London, it was surprising the number of famous buildings they'd never seen; no, it wasn't surprising, Wendy said: people rushed to Paris or Rome or Vienna and did all the tourist things, quite forgetting that their own back yard was of equal interest.

'So we'll be tourists then,' Kim said. 'The Monument for starters. St Paul's to follow, then what about the main course? The Tower?'

'I've changed my mind. I don't fancy the Monument,

and I've been to the Tower. I'd like to see some paintings.'

'The National Gallery?'

'No, something less exhausting. The Courtauld Institute.'

'Never heard of it.'

'It's by the University. It's not very big, and it has all the best Impressionists.'

'St Paul's then, followed by the Courtauld. Then a walk in Hyde Park; I want to crunch through the leaves.'

'You're a soft idiot!'

Neil, coming in and out of the kitchen, listened to all this with a rather sour look on his face; taking the hint, they dropped their voices in case he was hurt by what was being said. He was going to try some of the hostels again; she might have turned up somewhere since Saturday. There were two he had not been to, one because it was so far away, across the river in Peckham, and the YWCA, which he hadn't visited because it was so unlikely that Judith would go there. After that... he didn't know. He was going to have an evening off, bath, change, and meet some friends for a drink.

They went to the Courtauld first as it was nearer. Happiness bubbled in Kim like a spring; nothing could spoil today: it was out of time, enchanted. If he ran across the Tottenham Court Road without warning no cars would mow him down; they would part for him like the Red Sea for Moses. He did not put it to the test, however. And he reminded himself that what he had was fragile, compared with all that shared life that neither Wendy nor David would idly throw away, however roughly they sometimes treated it. But it seemed like a story he'd read, not real, nothing to do with today. He tried to summon up the self-pity he'd felt; he was just a kid, two months still to go to legal adulthood. Legal adultery Sandy Becker had called it. He was just a bit of extra. It didn't work; the bubbling happiness drowned out everything like that.

They cracked silly jokes, played childish games, giggled incessantly, running along the pavements and swinging on the lamp-posts. 'Lovers!' said a man, passing by, with a grin of mock disgust. 'How daft you are!' In the Courtauld they sobered up and walked slowly from one painting to the next, hands held together in Wendy's coat pocket. They absorbed Manet's *A bar at the Folies-Bergère*, Renoir's *La Loge*. Then the Modigliani nude.

'Well, you can take your eyes off her,' Wendy said. He did not respond. 'What's the matter?'

'Judith. It looks exactly like Judith. The head, bent over her left shoulder: Judith so often does that. And the hair; it's hers, absolutely.'

'Well, I wouldn't know,' Wendy said, a little acidly. 'I've not had the advantage of seeing Judith with no clothes on.'

'Neither have I. The figure's so... solid. Really there. Superb, isn't it!'

'David's just a bit taller than you; did I tell you that?' Wendy crinkled up her nose, trying to suppress a grin. 'Beautiful sun-tanned body. Sleek and fit.'

'Sleek and fit. Sounds like an advert for dog food.' He laughed. 'Look, it makes no difference.' They moved on to

Cézanne's *Lac d'Annecy.* 'Funny. I was thinking Judith *was* like that, not is. Almost as if she's dead.' Wendy did not answer. 'Perhaps she is. I mean metaphorically, dead inside me.'

'Well, that's probably good. For both of us.'

'She might literally be dead of course. I've thought of that. So has Neil, though we've hardly dared suggest it to each other.'

'There've been no reports on the news of any girls found battered or strangled.'

'No, there haven't. I think she's alive. In fact I'm sure she is.'

At St Paul's they started to argue again, but this time about the statue outside; was it Queen Anne or Queen Victoria? Anne; Wendy was right, and she added that she was old enough to remember seeing Churchill's funeral on the telly: on these steps the aged Clement Attlee had sat on a rickety wooden chair, an enormously impressive figure, the most memorable part of the whole performance, or so her dad had said. Kim would have been only five! Only five, just fancy! What connection, he wanted to know, did all this have with Queen Anne? St Paul's steps, she said; it all happens here. 'Female logic,' he muttered contemptuously, and that set them off on a squabble about women's rights which lasted the length and breadth of the cathedral's interior. Stereotyped roles, chauvinist attitudes, sexism (ridiculous word, Kim snorted; probably doesn't appear even in the biggest Oxford dictionary): yes, she went on, he was very conventional; doubtless he expected his future wife to provide him with three hot meals a day, wash and iron his clothes, always change the babies' nappies, always get up in the night if they cried. Why not, he answered, if he brought home the money, and, as she drew breath for another attack, said marriage and babies, he'd never given the matter a thought. Preventing babies was more his line of thinking. All he could envisage for the future was a warm loving relationship, not necessarily permanent, but which was a sharing of everything. One to one. He didn't want to imagine that every moment he couldn't be with her she might be having it off with an ex-boy-friend; he was trying very hard not to fall a prey once again to the horrors of possessiveness and jealousy. She stopped. They went up to the Whispering Gallery in silence.

'If it works out between us,' she said, 'if I think it really will work, I shan't see him. I promise. And I certainly won't go to bed with him.'

'Sssh! Not here! The echo goes all round and people will hear every single word!' He clung to the balustrade, giggling helplessly. 'I ... certainly ... won't ... go ... to ... bed ... with ... him!' he breathed, in an exaggerated stage whisper.

'Oh no!!' Her hand flew to her mouth and she blushed scarlet.

'I'm only joking. You have to speak close to the wall I think, if it's going to work properly.' He held out his hand. 'Listen.'

They leaned against the wall, but no clear words came to them. There was an immense continuous rustling, like the silk of thousands of old women's skirts, as if all the words spoken and whispered in the cathedral, all the muffled tramping of sightseers' feet, their coughs and incoherent murmurings, had collected here in a kind of mumbling meaningless jumble. Kim thought: the sound of silence. He looked across to the other side of the gallery, and his heart leaped inside him. Looking straight at him was Judith.

'Wait here,' he said, and ran. He bumped into people, apologized, and ran more quickly, for she was moving towards the exit. He dashed down the stairs, overtook her, and stopped, barring her way. She shrank back, frightened. It was his turn to blush scarlet. It was not Judith.

'I'm terribly sorry,' he said, gasping for breath. 'I really am very sorry if I frightened you.' The girl cried out in a foreign language; Italian or Spanish, he wasn't sure. She retreated, up the stairs. 'Look, I'm not trying to molest you or anything! I just mistook you for someone else, that's all! Oh, what's the use?' She evidently thought she was not at a safe distance from him, and turned and fled. Though he had to follow her to rejoin Wendy, he waited, not wishing to add to her distress. After a few minutes he ventured up, slowly. She was talking excitedly to another woman and an attendant, but fortunately she had her back to him. He slipped past and found Wendy.

'I think we'd better go,' he said. 'I might be on the point of being arrested for attempted rape.'

'Oh? Explain.' He did. 'Dear me! Judith does cause rather a lot of trouble, doesn't she?' She purred like a cat.

'Come on!' He tugged at her sleeve.

'There doesn't seem to be anyone official marching towards us,' she said, looking round. 'If her back was turned when you passed her she won't have seen you coming in here, surely? So if they're searching for a sex maniac like you they'll have gone down to the nave. I think we'd better stay where we are for a bit.'

He glanced about him. There was no sign of anything unusual. Reassured, he went to the balustrade and leaned over. The height was huge; people crossing the marble below were minute dots. The floor, he realized, was meant to be seen from the gallery rather than from ground level; only here could its symmetrical pattern of black and white show to full advantage. The proportions of it were exactly right. What a vast cylinder of empty space it was, this gap between the floor and the apex of the dome! He looked up at the painted figures on the inside of the roof, then back at the nave. And he began to remember details of what they had observed when they were walking down there, taken in only briefly because of their argument about women's rights; the memorial to John Donne, Holman Hunt's *Light of the World,* the ornate choir stalls, the simple clarity of most of the interior. There were no stained glass windows to cloud things with a gloomy richness, and the lack of monuments left the architecture uncluttered and pleasing to the eye. It's all so obviously what it ought to be, he decided, and he found himself wishing people were like that, himself, Wendy, Neil, Judith, clear and unmysterious.

They climbed up to where it was possible to walk round

the exterior of the dome and see London. Here all was clutter, a turmoil of buildings in all directions, modern rectangles of glass and concrete jostling with blackened Victorian brick, cranes and derricks marking the river, dull low hills to the north and south. The autumn sunshine and the blue dome of the sky made it all the more shabby, this great ferment that had been bubbling with human activity for nearly two thousand years: activity that seemed from here as tiny as the swarming of ants in an ant-hill.

They were just leaving the cathedral when the girl Kim had mistaken for Judith saw him. She and her companion pointed him out to an attendant in the doorway who shouted, 'Come back, you!' but he and Wendy ran down the steps and jumped on a number eleven bus that, most conveniently, happened to be passing. They stood on the platform, waving at the diminishing trio, until the bus carried them away, out of sight.

Monday found Mr Hooper still depressed. There's only one thing for it, he thought, as he gazed out of his office window at the dome of St Paul's: an afternoon away from here. The boss gave him permission and asked no questions; Mr Hooper had worked for Ashford and Penney, the City of London insurance firm, for most of his life, and had unexpectedly wanted time off no more than twice in the past eighteen years. He booked two tickets for a performance that evening of *Separate Tables* at the Apollo Theatre, then went home.

Beth was pleased, and rather amused. 'If an overnight

stay at Pevensey leads you into buying theatre tickets, we must do it more often!'

'It's not just that. I'm ... fed up.'

'Why? What's the matter?'

'I don't know. I seem to be missing Kim. Rather a lot.'

'He's been away from home before.'

'It's just this week-end ... Yes, he's in and out of this house every day, and perhaps we don't exchange more than a few words ... I've had this sense that we're losing him. That we've already lost him.'

'I don't know what you mean.'

'May be my imagination.'

'I thought he might have phoned, just for a chat. But he hasn't.'

'I'm bored, I suppose.'

'Oh?'

She looked as if she was going to take this personally. 'With myself,' he said. 'Bored with myself. It's all right when I've plenty to do ... the garden, tinkering about with the car ... but when I haven't ...'

'My women's magazines call it the male menopause. A very dangerous time, they say.' She smiled. 'One has to watch out for Signs of The Other Woman.'

'Oh, get on with you!' He stared at her. 'You don't really think that, do you?'

'No. I'm only teasing you. Idiot!'

They decided to drive up to town, and left early to avoid the worst of the rush. But traffic was at a standstill in Whitehall, so Mr Hooper went through the park, by

Birdcage Walk and Buckingham Palace. Then in Piccadilly it was one slow crawl.

'There's Kim!' Beth cried.

'Where?'

'Crossing at the lights!'

He had his arm round a girl; they were laughing and talking, faces nuzzled together, scarcely aware of the queue of cars about to accelerate as the lights went amber. When they reached the pavement, they stood against the glass front of a shop and he was kissing her. 'Making quite a meal of that, isn't he!' Mr Hooper muttered, as he drove on. He found the scene extraordinarily painful and was amazed at his reaction: stabs of pain inside, in his heart.

'Little liar!' Beth said, angrily. 'Says he's coming to London with some friend called Neil, and all the time it was a girl! I bet this Neil doesn't even exist!'

'I saw him, in the Globe. Well, I suppose it was him.'

'Exist he may, but he obviously isn't with Kim, is he! Just wait till I get hold of him! I'll give him a piece of my mind!'

'Neil?'

'Who do you think!'

'I shouldn't, if I were you.'

'Why not?'

'Let's discuss it later, shall we? We're nearly at the theatre.'

For Mr Hooper the evening was ruined. He felt so agitated he could hardly concentrate on the play. Beth seemed to be enjoying it. In the interval she talked about the act-ing, the set, how the plot was likely to develop when the curtain went up again. The incident with Kim, he guessed, had struck her chiefly as a piece of deception; she had been taken in, lied to. It could be dealt with at another time: she had probably worked out what she was going to say, and was looking forward to saying it. He, however, had experienced a very different set of responses, feelings so strange that for a while he was completely baffled. Halfway through the second act he began to realize what the emotion was: jealousy. He scoffed, inwardly, at the idea, but there was no doubt that it was true. It wasn't because the girl was physically attractive; he had caught only a brief glimpse of her, so he could not tell whether he would find her to his liking or not. Long blonde hair was all that had registered. No, it was the certain knowledge now of this other life his son was leading, an adult love-life, in which he and Beth and home had no part or significance. It was useless to remind himself that it was absolutely normal, that it was desirable that young people should grow up and fall in love; in this case it was happening without his ever having known his son properly, been close to him, been needed. And it was all his own fault.

Perhaps Kim had lied, perhaps not. It was possible he had told the truth about coming to London with Neil; maybe he'd only just met this girl, since he'd been here. Unlikely though. It was, on the face of it, deliberate dishonesty, but he didn't blame Kim for that in the way Beth did: what else could the boy do? Say 'Mum, I'm going off for a few nights to sleep with my girl-friend'?

The jealousy became almost wild as he thought of Kim making love to her. Why, why, he asked himself, should he feel like that? The answer stared at him quite plainly: because he had never done anything like that himself. How bloody lucky the young were, with their own culture, their own heroes, their own kind of clothes, the pill, the lack of restraint their elders imposed on them! Freedom! Freedom to be themselves. He'd never known it, and now it was too late. Too bloody late!

On the way home he said to himself he would try and get closer to Kim. If it was to be the last thing he ever did, he would try. He thought of his son with an almost fierce affection. He would *not* lose him! He couldn't say anything of this to Beth. She wouldn't begin to understand. It would all have to be bottled away, inside.

'Don't mention to Kim that we saw them,' he said.

'I most certainly will! Whatever are you talking about?'

'You will not. That's an order!'

'You aren't going to sit there and give me orders!'

'In this case I am. If you breathe a word of it I shall be extremely angry.'

She was bewildered. 'Cliff, why?'

He thought for a moment. 'What good do you think it will do?'

'I want to make it quite clear that I don't like being lied to. That I don't approve of my son spending three nights out with some strange girl we've never even heard of. Do *you* approve?'

'I don't think it's important whether I approve or not.'

'Cliff, I'm surprised at you! I know the younger generation has different views about everything, but there are limits!'

'I daresay there are. But just leave this particular matter alone!'

'I don't understand.'

'Have you ever asked yourself ... Oh, what's the use?'

'No. Go on. I'm listening.'

'Have you asked yourself why he should lie and deceive?'

'Tell me.'

'Because he doesn't trust us. Because we're not close to him. Because he can never come to us with a problem. Because, as far as this affair's concerned, the last thing on earth he could say is "I'm going to my girl-friend's for a few days".'

'Obviously!'

'You don't see the point. I tell you it doesn't matter if you like it or not. If you love someone enough there'll be a lot of things you won't approve of, but you'll accept them, just because you love that person. And I love my son.'

'I don't understand you.'

'Why do we keep making assumptions, anyway? All we saw was Kim in Piccadilly with a girl, when he's supposed to be with a boy. What a storm about nothing! Here we are, thinking they're sleeping together, when there may well be a perfectly innocent explanation. And what if they are? It's none of our business. We're behaving like two dirty old men!'

'It's the innocent explanation I want to hear.'

'You just try it . . . you try it, and I warn you, I'll never forgive you!' He sounded so violent that she was frightened into silence.

Later, in bed, she tried to re-open the discussion, but he wouldn't respond. She stroked his arm gently, but he turned away in disgust. There was nothing he wanted less, at that moment, than to make love to his wife.

SEVEN

Next day he was alone in the flat. There was little point in staying, for Wendy had returned to work and wouldn't be in until a quarter to six, and, as he was meant to be at school the following morning, he had to go home that night. But at least they would have a few hours together. Kim rang his mother and said he was catching a train that would get him back some time between half past ten and eleven.

'You sound a great deal more cheerful,' she said.

'I am.'

'Hmm.'

'You sound a bit edgy.'

'Not really. It's the weather, I imagine. I'll see you later.' She rang off.

He wondered what to do with himself to speed away the morning and the afternoon, and wished he'd brought his school books with him. There was plenty of work due in tomorrow that would have to be left uncompleted, and excuses to invent for why it had not been done. He found

Wendy's copy of the Simon and Garfunkel record. It's laughter and it's loving I disdain. I am a rock, I am an island! I'm not a rock, he said to himself; I'm not an island. I don't need this record any more. He switched it off.

He decided to clean out the flat; found dusters, the vacuum cleaner, furniture polish, Vim, and set to, pleased at the idea of saving Wendy the household chores. The time disappeared quickly; he was glad to be doing something active. He thought about the past few days as he dusted and swept. Judith and Neil, Wendy and Kim. It sounded like a happy foursome, that way of going out favoured by so many of his friends on a Friday or a Saturday night: the pleasure of parading your relationship in front of another; a bit of masculine talk with your mate while the girls went to the loo to pat their hair or gossip or whatever it was they found to occupy themselves with, endlessly, in there; dancing with your girl, and a couple of discreet dances—never more than two, for some unspecified reason, consecutively—with your mate's girl-friend, during which you wondered what on earth he thought was attractive in her, or else you lusted secretly, thinking she might be a much more interesting proposition than your own. Judith and Neil, Wendy and Kim. It would be nice, but it was quite impossible, of course.

Yesterday had been marvellous. They had walked in Hyde Park, though Wendy grumbled a bit, saying she'd had enough footslogging for one day. But, like him, she enjoyed the smell of the fallen leaves, the hazy sun, the ducks on the Serpentine. Later they flopped down in a café in Kensington High Street, drank tea and ate sticky iced cakes. In the evening, Neil went out as he'd said, and they had the flat to themselves. They stayed in and watched television. Idle chat, no arguments for once. They were in bed and almost asleep when Neil returned, a bit drunk they guessed, to judge by the heavy staggering movements round the kitchen. At breakfast he was complaining about a sore head and having to drive to work. After he'd gone Kim felt he should have said goodbye properly; Neil was going back to Purley that night, and they hadn't discussed when they would meet again. If at all. But he assumed they would: Neil would probably have said something if he'd felt a long time would pass without their seeing each other. The whole wretched business of Judith had been left so unsolved, had petered out so unsatisfactorily; Kim wanted to know what Neil intended to do now, whether he would go on searching at some future date, or try and forget her. Perhaps getting drunk last night was the first step towards putting her out of his mind.

His thoughts turned to Wendy. There were also unsolved problems there, of David, chiefly, but he was unsure of his own emotions as well. Was he in love with Wendy? He didn't know. If he was, it was very different from what he had felt for Judith. That, on the whole, was undoubtedly a good thing, but the problem was he didn't feel himself so involved. It wasn't intense; his whole life didn't depend on it. It was simply very enjoyable. What's wrong with that, he asked, and the answer was: nothing at all. But something would have to happen to test his feelings. He didn't know what, some crisis perhaps, so that he would be certain, so that he could say, yes, I love her; she means everything to me. Only then would the love-making seem right, make him feel totally happy. And was it satisfying for her? He wanted to ask how it compared with David, but her answer might not be quite honest. Then he thought of what their mouths and lips had discovered: real tenderness. He smiled, remembering a remark he'd read somewhere about one of the many differences between his own generation and his father's. Twenty years ago, young men's problems were about getting it at all; nowadays that was taken more or less for granted, and young men worried about how they were doing it. No-one was ever satisfied. He recalled other difficulties that some time ago had disappeared altogether, were evident nonsense, the kind of things you talked about with your mates when you were fifteen or sixteen, like was the size of it important, what would a girl think if it was too small; how often should you do it, would several times a week sap your strength; was there a grain of truth in those old stories about playing with yourself? All twaddle, proven rubbish. How you used it was more important than size; and he knew from his own experience that frequency, alone or otherwise, made no difference to his energy.

Sex; all his thinking seemed to revert to sex. He vigorously dusted a picture, and remembered his obsessive train of thought about how lucky he'd been all his life until developing sexuality had intruded and spoiled things, fixed him in that useless love for Judith. It was not true; it hadn't spoiled things, hadn't spoiled them at all. Just made life more complicated. And growing up was bound to be complicated, a blundering bewildering succession of experiences that was turning him from a safe happy child into the complex being called an adult, capable perhaps at last of coping, of choosing. Perhaps that was what he was, not a fixed known person with characteristics people could recognize as always being there, but a collection of memories and experiences. He was only the sum total of everything he'd been, and therefore always growing and developing. And somewhere, very difficult to see at seventeen or eighteen—or maybe at any age—in that collection was a pattern, a meaning.

The telephone rang. He picked up the receiver and gave the number. There was a slight pause, and a man's voice asked 'Is Wendy there?'

'No.' David! It must be! His skin prickled at the thought.

'They said at the estate agent's that she'd gone out, so I wondered if she'd come back to the flat for lunch.'

'She won't be in till a quarter to six.'

'Oh. Who's speaking?'

'Kim Hooper. I'm ... er ... a friend of her brother's.'

'Can you leave a message for her, please? Tell her I rang ... David ... and that I'll be round at about six.'

'I think ... she's busy this evening.'

'Is she? Doing what? Washing her hair?'

'I ... um ... I'm not sure.'

'Tell her I'll be there at six, please.'

'It ... it might be better if you came tomorrow.'

'Why?'

He hesitated. The arrogant voice was extremely annoying. 'I just feel it would, that's all.'

'That's for Wendy to decide, isn't it? Who are you, anyway?'

He knew he shouldn't say it, but he was angry. 'I don't think that's any of your business.'

'Maybe it is my business. Are you Neil's friend or Wendy's?'

'I happen to know them both.'

'Do you? Well, I've never heard of you. I think I'd better come over now.'

'What on earth for?'

There was a sound of mild irritation at the other end of the phone, then 'Tell Wendy I'll be there at six' and he rang off.

To ring Wendy was the obvious course of action, but Kim knew neither the name of the place where she worked nor its telephone number. He hunted through the yellow pages, but there were hundreds of estate agents; it would take hours to try them all. He was determined, however, not to be in the flat at six o'clock; in no circumstances did he want a confrontation with David. He had handled the conversation just now badly enough: a tremendous quarrel between David and Wendy was inevitable as a result of what had been said. He should simply have taken the message and rung off. He would probably get all the blame from Wendy; it might even jeopardize his chances with her, particularly if David knew exactly what to do to win her back. On the other hand, he thought, the phone conversation might have done some good. It was possible, now David knew there was somebody else, that he would be so angry it would make it easier for her to tell him to get out of her life. The main thing, though, Kim was certain, was that *he* should not be there this evening. It was something the two of them had to sort out alone; his presence would only make matters worse. He would write Wendy a note and leave as soon as he had finished cleaning the flat.

Did it look like running away, he wondered, as he tore up the first copy of his letter. Was it in fact running away, just an avoidance of a potentially unpleasant situation? Quite probably. He tried to stress in his letter that it was not. After three or four attempts he had composed something that he thought would do, and he put it on the hall table. He would ring her later that evening, he said. When he had finished sweeping the carpet he packed up his things and left. A disappointing end to the past two days, he thought, as he made his way to Victoria. Not with a bang but with a whimper: and he laughed inwardly at the unintended pun, thinking, yes, it was literally true.

He looked out of the train window at the drab streets of Battersea and Clapham. Clapham Junction, East Croydon, South Croydon, Purley Oaks and Purley, all familiar station names since childhood trips to London with his parents, then journeys, when older, with friends to football matches or those occasional aimless evenings in the West End, a gang of young teenagers together, drinking in coffee bars, gazing at the bright lights, scrutinizing the naughty pictures outside the clubs. This time had been very different. He felt remorseful; he had nearly forgotten Judith. He wondered where she was and what she was doing, but it was now almost the idle curiosity with which one might speculate over a long-lost friend; no, he said to himself, not so idle, but that, in a few weeks or a few months, was what it would be. He no longer loved her, not one bit. It surely couldn't have happened so suddenly. You couldn't be intensely in love with someone on Friday and feel nothing for her by Tuesday. Or could you? Certainly you might kid yourself you were in love, and when the scales dropped away from the eyes, you would know you hadn't wanted her as much as you imagined. That three weeks of jealousy: was it really because he'd needed Judith so much? Wasn't it perhaps the humiliation of being abandoned, the hurt to pride, the knowledge of being unimportant that had been the driving forces, not love? It was much easier to end an affair, to walk out on your partner, than be the one who was left, even if you both knew there was no point in carrying on: he'd seen that among his friends. It was very easy to mistake humiliation for thwarted love.

His one week with Judith had been far from happy. Looking back on it, he was able to tell himself that you could go on and on wanting something for years, but, eventually, if you didn't achieve it, the desire was bound to burn itself out. Perhaps he'd thought of her too much in the way you hoped to score the winning goal seconds before time. Love, he could see now, wasn't some kind of first past the post, or a trophy you put on the mantelpiece.

His mother was surprised to see him so early. She gave him tea, and cakes she had just made, still warm from the oven. 'Did you enjoy yourself?' she asked.

'Yes, thanks. Not bad.'

'What did you do?'

'Oh . . . went to St Paul's. Never been in there before. It's splendid! And the Courtauld Institute.'

'What's that?'

'An art gallery.'

'Oh.'

'How's Grandma?'

'Very upset. Biscuit's vanished.'

'Biscuit! What happened?'

'Dad saw him on Saturday afternoon, but he couldn't catch him. Grandma's afraid he's been run over.'

'Poor old cat. Poor old Gran, come to think of it.'

'She was disappointed not to see you.'

'Next time you go down.'

'What?'

'I'll come with you.'

'Yes, I think you'd better. Kim . . .'

'What?'

'Nothing. Would you get the washing in for me? It's just started to rain.'

At ten to six he rang Wendy. She was flustered, spoke so rapidly and in such a low voice that it was difficult to hear what she was saying; obviously David was already there and listening. She couldn't talk now, she said; she'd phone tomorrow. What was the number? He told her.

'Whatever happens,' he added, 'I'm seeing you at the weekend. I'm coming up on Friday, and I won't take no for an answer.'

'I *must* go.'

'Right.'

She rang off.

'Kim. Would you help me fix this sink?'

He shut his maths book and went into his parents' bedroom. He was surprised; he couldn't remember when Dad last wanted him to help with a job in the house. 'What's the problem?' he asked.

'I daresay I could manage it myself, but four hands are better than two. Can you hold the basin very firmly while I screw up this nut? I don't think Bill Meadows has given me the right spanner.' Mr Hooper, lying on the floor in a most uncomfortable position, worked in silence for a while, apart from some laboured breathing and several grunts. Then he said 'Turn the tap on, will you?' Kim did so. 'Blast it! Off! Bloody thing's still leaking.' He stood up and surveyed his handiwork.

'Let me give it a try.'

'O.K.' He wiped his hands on a rag.

Kim now grunted and heaved. 'It's shifted a little,' he said, panting. 'Turn on the tap.'

'You've done it!' The water was no longer seeping out of the joint. 'You're stronger than I thought.'

'Me big man, Daddy-oh.'

Mr Hooper grinned. 'Did you have a good time in London?'

'Yes. Dad ... I'm thinking of chucking in my Saturday job.'

'Why's that?'

'I may be a bit busy at the week-ends. I'm not sure yet, but if I am, I might take a job at the Oaks Café a couple of nights a week instead. Steve Taylor says they want an odd-job boy on Tuesdays and Thursdays.'

'What about your homework?'

'I can manage. It's eight till eleven thirty, so that leaves plenty of time after school to get things done.'

'What's all this about being busy at the week-ends?'

He looked at his father. There was a faint smile in the corners of Dad's eyes. He's guessed, Kim thought. Why not tell him? It was so hard somehow. And the longer he waited the harder it became, yet it was increasingly obvious he ought to say something. Mr Hooper walked towards the door, the smile disappearing.

'Dad. I met a girl in London. Neil ... that's the bloke I went up with ... his sister. That's where we stayed, at her flat.'

'Not the girl you mentioned last week?'

'No. No!'

'What's her name? Neil's sister, I mean.'

'Wendy.'

'So you ... er ... might be going up to London on Saturdays.'

Kim nodded. 'It's not at all certain yet. There's complications.'

'Ah. There always are. Another boy, I suppose.'

'How did you guess?'

'She has to sort that out first? And she's... she's important, this one?'

'Yes. Very.'

Mr Hooper's face broke into a wide smile of pleasure. 'We'll go down to the Globe and I'll buy you a drink.'

'Thanks. But... why?' He was puzzled.

'Oh... no special reason. I just feel like it.'

'Because I told you about Wendy?'

'Something to do with that, perhaps.'

Later that evening Mr Hooper was in the garage studying the inside of his car. It had not been ticking over too well, occasionally cutting out when the engine was idling. Dirt in the carburettor as like as not. He sang as he worked. *It's cherry pink and apple blossom white...*

Beth came in with a cup of tea. 'You're cheerful,' she said.

'I am. Where's Kim?'

'In his room catching up on his maths. What have you two been talking about, and why did you go down to the pub?'

'There is a girl. Her name is Wendy. She's Neil's sister. No, he didn't waltz off to London because of her. He met her there. And he's in love with her. He didn't say that last bit, but it's damned obvious to me that he is. No lies, you see? We got it completely wrong.'

'Oh.'

'For once you're at a loss for words.'

'Why couldn't he tell me all that?'

'I don't know.' He leaned into the engine and started to poke hard with a screwdriver. 'He's giving up his Saturday job, or, rather, he may be, so he can spend more time with her in London, and he's going to work during the week instead. Tuesdays and Thursdays. All I can say is she'd better be bloody marvellous. Because he's my son.'

'Really, Cliff! I'm not having him gallivanting off to London and spending every Friday night and Saturday night away from home! At his age!'

'You do leap to conclusions, don't you! He just said he might be busy at the week-ends. We were wrong once, so let's keep quiet, shall we? In fact, if you say one word I shall assault you with this screwdriver!'

The phone rang, and she went indoors to answer it. Kim had got there first. 'It's Grandma,' he said, handing her the receiver.

The cat had returned, safe and sound, not a mark on him. Hungry, that was all. She'd heard a faint mewing at the back door half an hour ago, then a scratching, and she'd gone outside, and there was Biscuit, large as life. Beth couldn't have any idea how thrilled she was to see him! It was wonderful!

Mrs Hooper hurried out to the garage to tell Cliff the good news.

'Oh, that's great,' he said. 'That's definitely made my evening, that has. My cup runneth over.'

'Why do you always have to be so sarcastic?'

He laughed and put his arms round her. 'Beth, I love you.'

'Hey! I'll get oil on my cardigan!'

'You're so predictable. And bugger the cardigan.' He kissed her.

EIGHT

It felt very odd next day, going back to school. The half-term had been such a leap into adulthood that putting on his blazer and tie seemed to belong to another Kim, one that had been left behind in the past. It was like clothing himself in a skin that had been shed. For the first time for some while, however, he was able to concentrate fully on his work, ask the right questions, and conduct an experiment in the physics lab with real care and attention. Mr Dobson noticed with a sort of ironic satisfaction; either the lad was no longer in love, he concluded, or else over half-term he had discovered what it was all about. It wasn't Judith now who produced the rush of blood, the slide in the stomach, but Wendy, the prospect of next week-end; those same sensations that last week were the result of emotional stress had become the signals of anticipated happiness. How will I live till then, he asked himself. David he deliberately put out of his head.

It was games that afternoon, and he thoroughly enjoyed his football, rushing about with such energy that the P.E. teacher said the holiday had obviously done him a world of good, and that he had been thinking of dropping Kim from the first eleven, his recent performances had been so poor. It didn't look as if that would be necessary now. Later, in the showers, he listened to his friends' crude jokes: after a game was always a time for more than usual coarseness. He wondered why. Girls became no more than holes and tits, boys' organs of incredible ability. It was as if they didn't exist as people who could think and feel. Perhaps it was all this collective male nudity that produced a sort of nervousness which needed obscenity as a cover-up or defence. Wearing clothes, and being in the presence of girls, as they were every other time of the week, was softening and civilizing, evidently a good.

Wendy rang him at about nine o'clock. It was an extremely unsatisfactory conversation, and he cursed whoever invented the telephone and himself for being so inept. Yes, she and David had rowed and fought all evening and almost all night, mainly because of Kim, but David would not accept that it was finished. He just refused to believe it.

'Did you say all night?' Kim asked.

She hesitated. 'Yes.'

'Where did he stay?'

'Here.'

'Yes, I know that. Where? On the sofa?'

'No.'

'In your bed?'

Again she hesitated. 'Yes.'

'And you were in the same bed?'

'There *is* only one bed. Kim, we didn't—'

'You expect me to believe that! I should be so stupid!'
'We did not do anything!'
'I don't believe you.'
'Oh, shut up!'
'Wendy.'
'What?'
'Is he coming round tonight?'
'I don't want him to, but he said he would. About ten.'
'Don't let him in.'
'I can't do that.'
'Why not?'
'Because I can't.'
'Because you want him to screw you; that's it, isn't it?' He knew he sounded hysterical; he knew he was ruining it all, but he couldn't stop himself. The idea of that man in her bed made him want to hit out at anything, her, himself, the whole flimsy world they had built over the weekend.

'If you're going to talk like that—'
'I can't stand it. Do you hear? I can't stand it! If you do it with him once more, if you did it last night, it's over between us. Right?'
'I won't be bullied by you or anyone! I'll work it out myself; do you mind? In my own way. Just keep out!'
'Yes. I know what your way is.'
'Kim—'
'Bed with both of us until you've—'
'Kim!'
'Fuck off!' He slammed the phone down.

He went into the living-room where his mother was

sewing buttons on a dress. He wondered, for one awful moment, if she'd heard any of the conversation, but the television was on, quite loudly. 'I'm going out for a bit,' he said.

'Wrap up well, dear. It's chilly now; soon be winter.'

'Yes, Mum.'

The night was cold and he wished he had put on his overcoat. He found himself treading the same familiar streets, automatically almost. It was anger that impelled him now, not jealousy; his step was not the shuffling gait of someone beaten and hangdog, but a stride full of energy. Unfortunate flowers growing near fences he decapitated like a karate expert. He felt angry with himself for the most part, but some of it was directed against Wendy. She was expecting too much, that he should stand idly in the background while she sorted out which of two men she preferred. What chance did he have if he didn't force her, issue ultimatums? All he had to offer was that he was new and different. David had nine years' start on him, nine years' experience of life, of how to deal with the opposite sex. Money and a car. The frustration of it, the waiting; to charge in like a bull in a china shop was an irresistible temptation, even if it smashed up everything.

He passed Judith's flat. The curtains were closed, but the lights were on. Her mother, probably, though it was strange; she worked evenings. Perhaps she had given up her job, or couldn't face it since her daughter had disappeared. He wondered if it could possibly be Judith herself, and there was a little flutter round his heart as he realized that it might just be that she was in there, a few yards from him. He stood undecided for a moment; should he go up and see? If it was only her mother, he ought to ring the bell anyway: she would want to hear the details of their attempts to find Judith. Or would she? They hadn't found Judith; the failure might only add to whatever grief she was feeling. Grief: it was unlikely she was experiencing that emotion, to judge from what he had learned of her life. A blow to pride, self-esteem; what do people think of me as a mother when they know my daughter's run away from home? But maybe he wronged her; maybe she did care, and care deeply. The quality of a relationship between parent and child didn't just depend on the parent, not when your girl was seventeen or eighteen, adult herself. You both had choice.

He walked away. Neil would have spoken to her mother, told her all that was necessary. Even if by some extraordinary chance it was Judith behind the curtains, he didn't want to see her. Never wanted to see her again. Let silence be the only thing left between them. He wanted Wendy. He thought of her, with a great flood of tenderness.

When he reached home he dialled her number. He would apologize; he'd been unfair, stupid and bad-mannered: could she forgive him? There was no answer. They had gone out, he supposed. Or were they making love . . . No, no! He banged his fist against his head. He must stop thinking that. Hello darkness, my old friend. And if they were, what of it? Was he going to remain utterly faithful to Wendy for the rest of his life? It was unlikely. Though he certainly would as long as their relationship lasted.

She'll be in touch, he told himself, if she really wants me. If not... well, it didn't matter, did it? It sounded hard, but it was true.

'I'm thinking of starting on Kim's room next,' Mr Hooper said.

'What do you mean, starting on it?' Beth was sitting in front of the fire, catching up on old magazines. 'It really is very irritating the television going wrong. I don't know how to amuse myself! I do hope the man comes tomorrow.' Soon after Kim had gone out the set had made a strange crackling noise; the picture faded to a dot, and no amount of twiddling the knobs or flicking with the power point would bring it back.

'Decorating, I meant. To bring the conversation round to where it began.'

'Sorry. But it *is* annoying!'

'It hasn't been touched for four years and it needs doing. That's what I was turning over in my mind when I was in there the other night; you know, when I couldn't sleep.'

'You weren't thinking that at all!'

'I was.'

'You were rambling on about Kim growing up and you getting old.'

'Perhaps.'

'Well, you're much happier now, I must admit. What was bothering you?'

'Nothing important. Kim being away; that triggered it off.'

'He still seems rather moody.'

'He's got woman trouble.'

'Woman trouble!' She laughed. 'You make him sound so grown up and mature!'

'This Wendy's three years older than he is. She has a boy-friend she's trying to finish with, so I gather. Kim isn't quite sure where he stands.'

'Did he tell you that?'

'How else would I know?'

'And he's in love with her?'

'Kim? Yes.'

'Well, these things never last long at his age. You'll see. It had better not interfere with his school work, though.'

'*He*'ll have to solve that one. We can't.'

'Oh well, I expect I shall like her. If he ever brings her home, that is.' She returned to her recipes in *Family Circle*. She'd been left out of all these confidences; she didn't know why. It hurt. However, it was an ill wind; talking to Kim had made Cliff more cheerful. That was something.

'He's going to help me with the decorating.'

'Kim? He's hopeless! He'll get the paint coming out of his ears.'

'He has to learn.'

'What colour scheme does he want?'

'Coffee, mostly. And the ceiling sandstone.'

'He'll need some new curtains, then.'

'Oh, by the way. A surprise for you.' He opened his wallet and showed her two theatre tickets. '*Something Afoot* at the Ambassadors, eight o'clock tomorrow night.'

'Twice in one week! Whatever's come over you? We don't normally go more than once in a blue moon!'

'I felt Monday was a disaster. I just couldn't concentrate. So I thought we should have another evening out, to make up for it.'

Kim came in, and sprawled on the rug in front of the fire. He was evidently in no hurry to go up to his room, but seemed to be enjoying himself teasing his mother about wigs and false teeth, bath chairs and walking sticks. It was an old routine, this, one that he had abandoned a year or two ago. It was always a question of how far he could press without upsetting her; there usually came a point when she stopped laughing and took offence. Tonight, however, he was careful not to say anything too rude, and she was not put out of humour. Mr Hooper went into the kitchen to wash up.

Kim followed, and helped himself to some cheese from the fridge. 'Since yesterday,' he said, 'we're ... I don't know ... closer.'

His father polished a plate, thoughtfully. 'I hope so.'

'I like it.'

'One day ... you must talk to Beth.'

'I want to. But it's ... difficult.'

'Try. Please.'

He looked non-committal. 'I'll put these milk bottles outside,' he said, 'then I'm going to bed.'

Well, Mr Hooper thought, at least his own little crisis was over, even if Kim's was not yet resolved. It was quite pathetic being jealous of the young. To keep in touch with them: that was more than adequate.

The next day, Thursday, passed. Kim was patient and excited. That's a paradox, he thought, remembering figures of speech from some tedious 'O' level English text book. No, oxymoron. Bitter sweet. Patient excitement. In his abstraction he dropped a glass beaker on the floor which smashed to tiny pieces. Mr Dobson frowned, told him to clear it up at once and wait behind at the end of the lesson. 'You're very erratic these days,' he said, when everyone else had gone. 'Your work's sometimes excellent, often just middling. Your mind doesn't seem to be on the essentials. What's the matter?'

'Nothing, sir.'

'All I can say is I hope she doesn't lead you much more of a dance. You're supposed to be one of my brightest hopes for a good 'A' level *and* a university place.'

'She, sir?'

Mr Dobson smiled. 'I can read the signs, lad.'

Kim blushed. 'It'll sort out, one way or the other. Tonight, I expect.'

'Well, I wish you luck.'

'Thank you, sir. If all's well, I promise you a grade one in June.'

'Get out. I want a grade one whatever happens. You can tell her that from me.'

He grinned. 'I will.'

On the way home he watched three dogs gambolling and chasing each other: they had such energy, such high spirits; they didn't have problems like humans did, daughters running away, drugs, conflicts of love and sex.

So long as there was somewhere warm to curl up and sleep, enough food to eat, they were happy. If there was such a thing as reincarnation, he thought he would like to come back as a dog.

Six o'clock, and Wendy would be in. Should he ring her at once, or wait and see if she rang him? Waiting was intolerable. His parents were out, their trip to the theatre; Mum had gone up to London and Dad was meeting her straight from work. He looked at his watch. Two minutes past six. He dialled the number. 'Wendy?'

'Kim. I'm sorry.'

'I am too. I said things . . . I shouldn't.'

'Me too.'

'How . . . how is it working out?'

'All right. Yes. It is. You're coming to stay for the weekend? No, there's no need to ask. You're coming!'

'You bet I am! But . . . there's one snag.'

'What? David won't be here.'

'Nothing to do with David. I have a Saturday job and I can't miss it again. I missed last week; I'd get the sack. And I'm broke. Those few days in London, they cost me every penny I had.'

'Doesn't matter.'

'I'll be with you Friday evening. We'll work Saturday out then. Anyway, I'm giving up the job after this week. I think. I can work Tuesdays and Thursdays instead. What happened . . . with David?'

'It's over. Really over. I've seen the last of him. I'll have to move; I won't be able to pay the rent on this place by myself.'

He paused, thinking absurdly he ought to commiserate. 'That's... bloody fantastic,' he said. 'When... er... er ... did he go?'

'This morning. Kim, nothing—'

'Don't tell me. I don't need to know. It doesn't matter if you did.'

'I love you, Kim.' He was too shocked to answer. 'Kim. Are you there?'

'Yes. Say... say it again. I can't believe it.'

'I love you, rat-bag.'

'Christ. Oh, Christ.' He seemed to explode inside. Yes, it was true, just as true for him. He knew, was as certain as anything he'd ever known. 'Wendy.' But it was so hard, curiously, to say it.

'You don't. Is that it?'

'Oh, no, no, no! I want you, I need you! I'll make you happy, I'll give you... I *love* you!'

'You're beginning to sound incoherent.'

'Don't... don't mock. I'm... trembling! Sort of weak at the knees! What are you doing, now, this minute?'

'Nothing.'

'Right. You just get on the first train and come here. At once. And stay with us tonight. Mum and Dad won't mind.'

'I'm sure they would!'

'In the spare room, I mean!'

'I don't know where you live.'

He explained, said he'd meet her at the station in an hour. 'Wendy. No, there's nothing to say. Just I love you!'

'I'll be there. In an hour.'

He raced up to his bedroom, dancing with delight: he needed music, what should it be? He threw Simon and Garfunkel under the bed, found the 1812 Overture. Fireworks, cannons, the Kremlin bells, an orgy of rejoicing; it was all bursting inside him, joy, joy, joy.